————————— ★ —————————

DESIRED EFFECT

The words were clear. WE WANT JUSTICE, in large capital letters, spread across the entire page.

"One of them told me this would happen."

"Lydia, what are you talking about?"

"First I thought he was trying to be kind. Offhand kindness to counteract their hostility. But now I realize. There was nothing offhand about it at all. It was a deadly serious message. He was telling me they'd do something terrible, but if I kept cool, then things would work out all right...."

————————— ★ —————————

UNDUE INFLUENCE

Miriam Borgenicht

TORONTO • NEW YORK • LONDON • PARIS
AMSTERDAM • STOCKHOLM • HAMBURG
ATHENS • MILAN • TOKYO • SYDNEY

UNDUE INFLUENCE

A Worldwide Mystery/December 1990

First published by St. Martin's Press Incorporated.

ISBN 0-373-26062-8

UNDUE INFLUENCE

WHEN THE CAR TURNED into the parking lot, the head-lights shone briefly on the high school. The rough stone, the tall arched windows, the recessed doorway that every morning proved inadequate for the two dozen students who wanted to go through it at once. The car in its headstrong course seemed headed for that doorway; as it moved closer, the girl could see the knob on the wooden door and the gates that as a matter of necessity had been put up within the past couple of years around it. But at the last instant, the driver swerved and headed left, into the long expanse of concrete bounded by a chain-link fence. No other cars impeded him as he drove along the diagonal painted lines; a sign in front said that cars left here overnight would be towed away at the owner's expense, and evidently it was a warning to be taken seriously. An impediment at the end, though; a large pile of sand for some future construction; over it the contractor had draped a plastic cloth which either a strong wind or the depredation of playing children had dislodged—half of it was spread on the ground, where the driver slipped on it when he opened the car door and stepped out. He regained his footing fast; enough, at any rate, to brace himself as he tugged at the girl. Standing with feet apart, he got a firm fix under her arms so he could slide her along the seat and then, head first, her hair streaming, to the ground. "Don't scream," he said. "I won't hurt you if you don't scream." She was incapable of screaming; the rigidity of her body seemed to extend to her throat, her mouth, her breathing.

It was that rigidity that infuriated him most; a short slender girl, but as she lay there, nothing about her was approachable, pliant. When he kneeled down to push at her clothes, he encountered first one layer and then another of disobliging material that trapped his hand in their filmy folds; he felt his knees scrape on the concrete without having advanced his purpose. His motions grew more frantic. "Help me," he muttered. She didn't help; she lay stiffly, a stick, a mummy, as if to taunt him, mock him. A cool March night, but his palms were wet; when he reached out to the nearby mountain of sand perhaps it was to rub some on his hand, give them more purchase on her resistant limbs. But his hand encountered a brick, one of the Belgian paving bricks with which the contractor was planning to line the newly dug tree pits over by the athletic field. It felt solid, reassuring; he picked it up to swat at her hands, which in their ineffectual way were beginning to claw at him. Instead, it smashed into her face. Ah. Something pliant at last. He brought the brick down again, and then, satisfyingly, a third time. Then he went about his business.

ONE

"Hey, Lydia, come in when you have a chance." Ben's big head, like a shaggy ball, bounced in and out of the door to her office.

She pushed back the papers on her desk. She liked that. A boss who doesn't stand on ceremony, tell his secretary to tell her secretary that Miss Ness is wanted. On the other hand, he expected others to read the clues, discern the special urgency behind the offhand clause. When you have a chance: Put down whatever the hell you're working on and get in here.

In his office, she pulled up a chair. Not the low leather chair he assigned to clients, so while they considered themselves reveling in comfort they also found themselves in a position three or four inches below that of their attorney.

"What's up, Ben?"

"You very busy?"

Another statement meant for discerning reading. As one who kept a vigilant finger on the activities of everyone in the firm, of course he knew she had to get the brief about the Stanhope case out by noon tomorrow.

"Got a big case for you, Lydia."

"I could use a big case. Soon as I get them to give that no-good Stanhope fellow back his license."

"You won't like this one."

She looked for a second at the pictures of children from his three marriages scattered indiscriminately around his desk. "The case or the client?"

"Neither one."

Well, "like." Not the most apt word to characterize one's feelings for most of Ben's clients. The affluent drug dealers, the bank presidents who had schooled themselves not to notice that money was being laundered down the hall, the arsonists, the respected professors found with pornographic material in the back drawers of their desks. And surely not the drunk drivers; how could you like the fact that because of some astute legal maneuvering on your part, a rich twerp who took the wheel of his expensive Italian car after drinking all night was going to get a crack at doing the same thing next weekend?

She doesn't much like them; she knows in advance she is not going to like them. "What's the case?"

"Jerry Eldstrom."

"Who's he?"

"Christ, Lydia, don't you read the newspapers?"

Well. Let's examine that good question in detail. When is she to read the papers? Between seven and eight in the morning, when she dresses Addie, feeds her, tries to make it seem against all the evidence that she isn't rushing her? Eight to eight-thirty, when she takes Addie to nursery school and vies with half a dozen other mothers for one of those two-minute conferences that will detail for a teacher the changes since the day before in temperament or dietary preferences or sleeping habits that seem to her indispensable data for one taking care of her child? Eight-thirty to nine, when those standing on either side of her on the subway are also attempting to turn to a particular page of the second section of their papers? Or does Ben perhaps mean evening, that interval between six and let's say eleven, when an uninterrupted hour with Addie, a quick dinner, an attentiveness to hair and complexion, and the final touches on a next day's summation all claim absolute priority?

Does she read the papers? "Sometimes yes, sometimes no."

"This was three months ago."

"Eldstrom, did you say?" She shook her head.

"That girl out on Long Island," Ben went on. "You know. They found her in a corner of a high school parking lot. Underneath some construction stuff. Her face had been—"

"Good God. Not that one."

"I thought you'd remember," he said with some delicacy.

"Ben, she was raped."

"Right. First he raped her, then he bashed her head in. Or the other way around, the medical examiner says he can't tell for sure."

"And you want me to defend the guy who did it?"

"I want you to defend the chief suspect. Or rather his parents want it. Good respectable people. The mother teaches shorthand at some secretarial school. The father is a pharmacist who owns his own drugstore. They were here yesterday making a pitch for their son. I'd have introduced you, but you were out."

Listen. I won't do it. There's no way you can make me. Murder, arson, drunk driving, robbing widows and orphans—okay. But rape—forget it. I absolutely will not take it on.... She was silent.

Ben was watching her. "What's your problem, Lydia?" he said. "You always wanted a case in the big time. You can't get much bigger than this. If he loses, he gets twenty-five to life; no one gives less for rape and murder. So you have your stakes—why are you complaining?"

"Three months ago," was all she said. "If they're such pillars of respectability, how come they didn't get a lawyer before this?"

"They did. But they don't like the way he's handling the case. Either that or someone told them I was the best—I didn't get it straight."

Benjamin H. Lyttle: when it came to criminal law, he was the best. She didn't have to agree to it, and he didn't require her corroboration. Let there be any kind of case with a twist—a battered wife kills her husband, a robber hits only teen-age girls—and his office gets the call. "But I can't take on anything in the next two weeks," he continued, "not with the Lenox trial coming up. So we tossed it around a little, me and those two distraught parents, and we came up with an idea. If a woman attorney defends him, a young good-looking woman attorney, if she will actually take the case, that can go a long way toward establishing an aura of innocence."

She had to smile. He means he came up with the idea and sold it to that luckless couple. His own thinking would have been more sophisticated. The case obviously needs a lawyer who knows how to put on defense witnesses—a job she was never called on to do at Legal Aid, where defense witnesses rarely exist, and one that for Ben's practice she has to bone up on. So that's Ben. A triple swoop: convince a family, win a case, and train his crack new lawyer in the bargain.

"I gave them some of your credentials. The tally of cases you've won." When he leaned forward, the hair that he wore long and did not have to dye fell around his ruddy cheeks. "Also, something else. You'll have to hustle. The trial's set for two weeks hence."

"Two weeks to prepare a case of rape and murder? How about the motion practice, the discovery? What do I do, rely on the first lawyer's work? How do we know what he was doing? Maybe he's a dimwit who missed half the legal issues, and we're stuck with his disaster."

"I told them only someone as bright and able as you could possibly—"

Ben and his smooth talk. "Ben, it's outlandish. It doesn't make sense."

"Tony will be helping you full time. He's young, I admit, but very snappy. He'll work twelve hours straight to find out the color of a pair of shoelaces. If what someone happens to need to know is the color of shoelaces." The phone rang, and he told his secretary whoever it was he couldn't talk now. "I also explained to those people that under normal circumstances you'd be reluctant to defend someone on a rape charge."

"This sounds normal enough to me," she said. "He rapes her, kills her, does an inept job of hiding her under a pile of sand. For that category of crime, everything standard."

"Those parents with an unshakable conviction of their son's innocence, they're not your standard mom and pop."

"I suppose he has an airtight alibi," she said wearily. "Three good friends who were with him that night."

Ben got up from his imperious chair. "Lydia, I know you don't care for it. It wounds your sensibilities. Offends your principles. Violates all those feminist values you rightfully insist on. Believe me, I understand." His tone was sincere but brisk, as if by having been fair enough to state her objections he had disposed of them.

It was the way he led witnesses on in court, agreeing with them, affably seeing their point of view, flattering their capacity for shrewd analysis, until numb, dazzled, they found themselves giving him the incriminating statement he was after. She shifted slightly so her head was further from his. There was no such thing as just meeting this fellow on a trial basis. Once Ben made up his mind, she was hooked. Wrong. When for her own reasons she had taken a job six months earlier in the firm of Benjamin H. Lyttle, she was hooked.

"I suppose there's a mint of money," she said.

"Actually, no. Those people live in Pendil Park. Town out on Long Island. You don't know it? No, why should you? You never met anyone from it, probably never heard of it. Me, I remember when some developer made a big splash about building it some forty years ago. Just about the time you were learning to read Dick and Jane. An exercise in construction efficiency, it was called: acres and acres of one-family houses, all with the same dreary front yard, unappetizing backyard, built-in amenities, sensible floor plans." The sonorous voice rolled out; she might have been an audience of fifty. "Urban designers shook their heads. Such mediocrity. Such conformity. Such an absence of civilizing touches—one generation and it would be a slum. Well, you know what? Those planners were wrong. The people planted trees. They looked at the color of their neighbors' house and painted theirs a different color. They built sunrooms and decks and back fences. And they do all right for themselves. They buy fur coats. They send their kids to college—not any college Lydia Ness would be seen dead at, maybe, but places that have gyms and libraries, hand out degrees. A mint of money? No. But they cling with ferocity to one of those lower rungs of the middle class. Ditto, incidentally, for the family of the victim, who come from a town about fifteen miles away."

The deep-set eyes were mellow; making a speech gave him the same sense of well-being that a good meal or a long drink could give to someone else. It was a sense with which an appreciative world provided him often, and not just when he was engaged in the line of duty. Let any controversial event be in progress, and it was in front of Ben Lyttle that the microphones were shoved. What did he think? Who was to blame? How would it all turn out? The reporters might not care for his opinions, sometimes they actively disliked them, but they knew their editors would print them. Even more, they knew an opinion would be forthcoming.

Something glib, newsworthy, sensational, welling up from that massive ego and fluent tongue.

"If those Eldstrom people aren't rich, how are they going to pay the fee you're accustomed to?" she asked.

"They mortgaged their house. Two mortgages. The first to cover bail."

"With all that middle-class respectability, why'd you say I wouldn't like them? Forgetting about rape and murder, of course."

"What I meant was, you wouldn't excuse them the way you did your Legal Aid clients."

She could feel herself bridling. When he referred to the job she held before this, there was always that suggestion of irony. "I put on my best act for them. That doesn't mean I excuse them."

"Sorry, Lydia," he said smoothly. "What I meant was, you had a rationalization for what they did. That nineteen-year-old who committed armed robbery—his father was in jail, or his foster mother beat him, or he watched his sister die of an overdose. And our affluent clients, their very wealth—yes, it's true—confers a kind of grace, provides another sort of rationalization. Something about the culture of greed, the syndrome of possessiveness being bred in." He paused, but not for her assessment. "But this Eldstrom fellow, no extenuating circumstances can be offered to explain him. From all I could make out in that single interview, two adoring parents think the world of him; without any particular training or talents, he makes a decent living; he has a girl friend who would marry him tomorrow. So if you're looking for excuses for his malfeasance—"

"But I thought the point was there is no malfeasance. He's innocent."

Ben gave her a sidelong glance. "That's my Lydia. On the button."

Back in her own office, she sat silent. You always tell yourself the worst thing won't happen, but it does, it does. "You really said yes to Benjamin Lyttle," her friend—her good friend—Douglas had said to her when she took the job. "Great thing is, he said yes to me." "Listen, Lydia. I thought you were doing fine at Legal Aid." "I was doing fine at Legal Aid. I just want what Lyttle can pay me." And when there was no softening of that stolid expression, "Doug, I know you think it's frivolous of me, but I want to buy expensive clothes. Really expensive. I want to re-cover my couch with some million-dollar fabric. I want Addie's room fixed up like those showplace rooms for little girls you see in the magazines. I know you don't care to think that about me, but these are things I really want." In fact, I want to be one of those women who live in New York without ever having to inquire about the price tag, his condemnatory silence discouraged her from adding. He didn't have to talk; his dogged, sincere face, crumpled with disapproval, said everything. Douglas was an engineer who advised builders on stress analysis, a profession that in his mind was imbued with mystic significance. Take care of the structure and the frills won't matter, was Douglas's dictum to someone who wanted to know the feasibility of incorporating green tinted glass or a carved cornice into a structure. Lydia's expensive wardrobe and redecorated couch plainly had the low standing of these inconsequential frills.

"All the thousands of law firms in this city," Douglas said. "They don't need me," she told him. "They need someone who knows about corporate mergers. After five years with Legal Aid, what I know is how to tell the jury they have the wrong man, it's someone else who held up the parking attendant." "You could learn about mergers." "They don't pay you for learning. Not much, anyhow." "If you'd marry me, you wouldn't need so much."

Lydia sighed. She might have known it would get around to this. Whatever the course of their conversations, there was always the point at which they got around to this. "Lydia, think it over," he said with his quiet insistence. "Marriage, I mean. You know? That good old-fashioned institution." "I tried it once. It had some bad effects. I need time to get over it." "You make it sound like a disease." That was not so far wrong. Marriage to Owen: a debilitating disease, the aftereffects of which call for a lengthy period of convalescence.

But in fact, though she has no intention of saying so, she sometimes thinks marriage to Doug would be just the thing for her. His stability, his reasonableness, his impermeable resolve. The truth is, she didn't leave Legal Aid simply for the chance at a larger paycheck. Oh, she likes the money, she has no trouble deciding how to spend it, but she also felt the need of new battles. She wanted to test herself against someone as splashy and celebrated as Ben Lyttle. After five years, she wanted to take a risk, and risk-taking is the one thing that is anathema to Douglas. Risk-taking means putting in an eyebeam of less weight than the specifications call for, it means letting a client build a cantilevered terrace six inches farther out than the most stringent rules suggest. It means that someday, maybe not in this generation but in another, something will crash. Lydia thinks of this prudence in tandem with her daring, and the combination seems to her a good one.

But since she knew better than to voice this opinion, Douglas didn't now press the desirability of marriage, but simply went on to the undesirability of Lyttle. "Someone with his dubious reputation," he said. "His reputation is that he wins," she pointed out. "Lydia, you may not like the methods by which he does so." "Oh, I don't know. Working for one of the most famous criminal lawyers in New York could be sort of fun," she said. "Defending murderers and rapists—Lydia, you call that fun?" "Come on, Doug. He keeps those plums for himself. He'd never turn anyone of that elevated culpability over to me." "Anyhow, there are worse than rapists and murderers," Doug said. "Who's that?" "The white-collar crooks," he said in his doggedly sententious way. "The ones who sit in their paneled offices setting up the deals in which a few thousand unsuspecting dupes lose their shirts. No, the worst is that Lyttle gets them off. They pay his fees and they're back in the paneled rooms cooking up the next deal." "If Ben didn't defend them, someone else would," she inadequately said. "Lyddy, don't do it. You'll hate it." "Don't worry. If I hate it, I'll quit. I promise."

She has no intention of quitting. What he doesn't understand, that nice Doug with his right-minded concerns, is that pride in craftsmanship operates independent of assessment of client. When she stands in front of a jury, there's always that moment when she doesn't think, This poor guy had a rotten childhood, or, He deserves a break, or even, What I do will make a difference for the rest of his life. What she thinks is that it's Lydia Ness against the prosecution. They have the cops, they have respectability, they have complaints, they have experts, they even have the facts. What she has is an uncooperative client in an ill-fitting suit. It's her guile against their airtight case. That's the picture she sees. Herself beating them by being smart.

It's the picture she sees now. She's wearing one of the suits that her new salary makes possible, and her hair is cut in the way suggested by the salon where she now has a weekly appointment, and her voice rings out with the clarity that used to win debates at college. "Ladies and gentlemen," she says. "You've heard the prosecutor give his version of what happened. I'm sure he believes this account. He means every word. But he doesn't know if it's true or not. How can he? He wasn't there. He didn't see, didn't hear. Which means that the version of the facts he just gave isn't evidence, any more than the very different version I'm going to give. The only evidence is what you're going to hear from people up there in the witness stand. Your job is to listen carefully to this evidence, weigh it, judge those who offer it. And I think when you've done that you'll say that the presumption of innocence has not been overthrown by the prosecutor. In other words, your verdict will be not guilty.''

How many times she's given that statement, or an approximation thereof, while the jury, still fresh at this early stage, leans forward with attentive stares, and the prosecutor ostentatiously scribbles himself a note, and the defendant sits nearby looking sheepish or defiant or abject or just plain confused. Then she remembered. Next time she gives that speech, the defendant will be someone who may have raped and killed a girl.

TWO

"So, Mr. Eldstrom, tell me about yourself."

"At the store, they call me Jerry."

"All right, it'll be Jerry. I still want to hear."

"Nothing much to tell. I work at Neils' Hardware, and I knew Pam, and I didn't kill her."

He was in her office, a tall, fair-haired, fair-skinned young man who sat, stood up, sat again as he delivered his curt answers. She was not surprised at the curtness; she'd met its counterpart before. Part of it, of course, signified his panic at the hole he was in, but added to that was the discomfort of a man who finds that the one designated to get him out of that hole is a woman. The lawyer who's going to defend him in a rape case is a woman. Presumably his parents had told him about the setup and he'd agreed to it, or he wouldn't be here, but still, there it was. Resentment, awkwardness, unease, making the start of this difficult interview still harder.

"Jerry, they have you on two counts of second-degree murder: intentional murder and felony murder. Felony because it happened during a rape, intentional—well, that's self-evident. Against this, we have only one defense. You. Your character. How good you are. If I'm going to make the best possible case for you, I have to know you better."

He stood again. "It's all in the papers. I have an apartment—one floor, really—in this house in North Rainey. I moved there four years ago when I started working for Neils'. I go home on Sundays to see my parents. I can't tell you about the crime because, like I said, I wasn't there."

She didn't need him to tell her about the crime; by noon, she had read all the clippings. Then Tony brought her copies of the first lawyer's records—police reports, autopsy reports, witnesses' statements, Jerry's first statements—and she read those. Now, at three in the afternoon, she had the general outline. After having been missing for almost a day, a girl called Pamela Howells was found imperfectly hidden under some construction material in a corner of the North Rainey High School parking lot. She had been imperfectly raped, too; that is, in the unsavory language of newspaper reporters, though there was hemorrhaging, and semen was found in her pubic hair, penetration had not been effected. After raping her, or possibly before—"There can be no certainty": the medical examiner—the murderer had taken a paving block from a nearby pile and bashed her face in so the features were—more unsavory language—indecipherable. A passerby had noticed an old green car driving out of the parking lot at about eleven-thirty, and because nothing was going on in the high school that night and a campaign had discouraged the teenage couples who used to park there, he took the trouble to look closely. Closely enough, anyhow, to remember that the first two numbers of the license were 29.

On the night of her death, Pam was nineteen years old, the youngest in a family of ten brothers and sisters. She'd graduated from high school two years before, and since then she'd been living with her parents at 28 Oak Lane, which was a quiet street of one-family houses in North Rainey. She had no job. She attended no school. Except for occasional stints of babysitting for the children of her siblings, she stayed home, keeping busy with the small domestic chores like cleaning and cooking. During the past month or so, however, she'd been engaged in a rather larger chore: redoing her bedroom.

It was how she met Jerry Eldstrom. About five weeks before her death, she came to Neils' Hardware with questions about her project, and Jerry was the one who waited on her. After that first visit, she went several times, always consulting with Jerry and only Jerry, waiting for him if he was busy, going away and coming back later if he happened to be out. Once, when she had bought two gallons of something and didn't care to wait for a delivery until the next day, Jerry drove her home. On the night of her death, a couple of her married sisters were visiting, and they heard Pam say "Jerry?" in a tone of pleased surprise when she answered the phone. When she told her sisters she was going out to meet a friend, they were the surprised ones because her social life had always been so limited. But they were accepting about it. One sister—her name was Stacy—told her to wear a plaid scarf rather than that old blue one, and the other said why didn't she put on nicer shoes. They never saw her again.

Once the body was discovered, it took the police only a few hours to find out that the Jerry Eldstrom who worked at Neils' had an old green car with a license number that started with the numbers 29. He denied that he'd called Pam or seen her, indeed he said that from eight o'clock that evening he'd been with his girl friend, Fern Eaton. He was arrested, and a week later he was indicted by the grand jury.

That was all except for the attempts to sketch some kind of personality for the main participants. What was Pam like, this girl whose life had ended with such cruel abruptness? It's hard to get a fix from a bereaved family; understandably, they're devastated, incoherent, prone to exaggerated adulation: the desire for deification goes along with the need for vengeance. In this case, however, because of the limited nature of Pam's life, the family members were the only ones in position to testify. According to them, she was a saint, a paragon, an exemplar of sweetness, their beloved sister. But reading carefully, you also got a picture of someone retiring, shy, unobtrusive—perhaps, Lydia wondered, slightly backward? Even retarded? And of course there were the facts. All the rest of that large family, along with their spouses, seemed to lead full and energetic lives; they were electricians, dental hygienists, nurses, truck drivers, insurance salesmen, florists—one brother was a man to know inasmuch as he administered tests for those seeking driver's licenses. Also, far from sticking close to North Rainey, they had addresses ranging from Bridgeport, Connecticut, to Rockville, Maryland. And they had families of their own; one sister—the florist—was pictured with her three children dabbing at red eyes as they assimilated the news about Aunt Pam; two others were photographed leading somberly attired groups of boys and girls into the church for the funeral. Pam, then, was not following family tradition when she chose to restrict her days to that maidenly bedroom.

As for the young man singled out to help redecorate that room, you got a picture of someone affable, easygoing, ingratiating—the kind a customer would naturally gravitate to on walking into a bustling store. He had no criminal record, not even a speeding ticket, he went out with an appreciative young woman, he was well liked by the other salesman.

Lydia sat for a long time with the clippings. She had little experience at having her trials publicized. At Legal Aid, the cases she handled were rarely the stuff of newspaper headlines. A sixteen-year-old arrested for the third time with a stolen car radio, a supermarket checker assaulted, a drunken fight that ends in the emergency room…these translated into statistics, into lists, into editorials, depending on where one was sitting, about the need for stiffer sentences or the callousness of the system. They were cause for general dismay but not significant enough for individual accounting. But something about the hideousness of this particular crime or, as Ben said, the unremitting respectability of the players struck a collective nerve; poor Pam, who had rarely ventured down her porch steps and engaged in few dealings with anyone beyond them, was pictured on various front pages for three days running, while Jerry's round, rather ordinary face was photographed from angles calculated to make it look interesting and sinister.

He didn't look sinister now. He looked troubled and earnest and angry. But also when he talked, his eyes radiated the kind of eagerness that could mask a craftily aggressive nature but could also denote exactly what it appeared to, which was a man whose natural inclination was to please.

This time when she said again she wanted to hear about him, he started right in. "I'm a salesman at Neils' Hardware—I guess you know that. Been there since high school. First I thought I'd go on to electronics school, my father was rooting for it, but I got this summer job at Neils' and you know how it is. It gets to be September and things are going all right, so why rock the boat—it's over four years now. In another year, Old Man Neils might let me buy an interest in the business. He hasn't put it in writing, but I think he means it. And neither of his sons is interested—one's a dentist, the other is in insurance."

The voice was more relaxed. Nothing to tell, he'd said, but now that he'd started, the words had their own momentum. It always happened. First she was that person of unsuitable gender on the other side of the desk, then she was defense counsel, then the category broadened to include confessor, helpmate, friend. He liked the business, he said. Selling hardware—not just a matter of taking down paint cans from the shelves. You had to bone up on the products, know what was applicable and what wasn't. Say a man comes in with a problem, like he's just spent three days caulking his windows and there's still a draft. You have to analyze it. The walls, the exposure, the type glass, the internal conditions. Sort of like being a doctor. Figure out the ailment and then treat it. And they get to trust you. They know you're pushing a product because it's good, not because you get a rake-off. Ask any of the contractors who come in—lots of times he knows more about solving their problems than they do.

Pride colored the account. Pride, youthful arrogance, enthusiasm—a young man geared to please others and also pleased with himself. Then the tone darkened: a young man also, and don't forget it, under indictment for rape and murder. Pam having a problem, that was how he got to meet her, he said. She wanted to paint her bedroom, but there was old wallpaper. Two, maybe three layers, what should she do about it?

When he went over to the window, Lydia appropriated the view through his fresh gaze. The clumps of skyscrapers, the single church steeple, the scaffolding for a new building even taller than the surrounding ones, all topped, this June day, by a cloudless blue sky that seemed to belong to a different world from this air-conditioned office.

"A girl like that, fifteen years old, I figured she wouldn't stay in the bedroom long. I said paint over the wallpaper. Any loose edges, you get wallpaper paste and stick them back on. What plenty of people do. Job lasts maybe four years, by then she'd have left home, let somebody else have the headache. But she said no, it was her room, her room for keeps, she wants to do the job right." A small grimace crossed the open face. "So I sold her some chemical stripper and gave her the standard precautions. You know. Windows open, wear gloves, put something over her hair, quit right away if she feels a headache or nauseous or anything. What anyone can find out just from reading the instructions."

"But you took the trouble to tell her."

"I take the trouble with lots of customers," he said. He came back and sat down, but the tone was the same: eagerness tinged by perplexity. A week or so later, he said, the girl came back. He was busy, and she stood around waiting for him. She wanted to report. She'd taken off the wallpaper, it was hard work, all that dirt and dust and scraping, but she managed, and guess what. She took a picture to show him. As if, he said bitterly, he was some kind of goddamned teacher or something. Anyhow, she wanted to know what was next, so he told her she had to get the wall smooth. No cracks anyplace.

"I sold her a spackling knife and some all-purpose spackle, and told her how to apply it. Wet the cracks with a sponge, pack in the filler, then wipe off with a damp rag just after the paste begins to set. Maybe five or ten minutes. The usual tip if you want to skip doing the sanding, which is a big nuisance and no one has the patience to do it right anyhow. And if there's a big cavity, maybe she'd have to fill it in two or three stages, giving each layer time to harden."

He looked up, as if surprised at his own voice; he'd been carried away by his disquisition. After that, he went on, she kept coming in for instruction or consultation or whatever. She didn't ask for him, she didn't have to. The other clerks all knew. Hey, Jerry, your customer is here, they would say with sly amusement.

Lydia nodded; she suddenly remembered that when she was in high school she'd been in love with a boy like Jerry. The fair hair and skin, the lanky body, the well-intentioned manner, the open face. His name was Ed, and the only trouble was, her best friend Sharon went out with him. She herself went out with a boy who was very different: short, dark, secretive, intense. Long after she became impatient with Sharon's plaintive ways and boring talk, she kept the friendship intact so that if Sharon and Ed showed signs of breaking up, she would be the first to know. They never did break up. She could picture them now, dancing at the senior prom, Sharon's moony head on Ed's shoulder where her own was longing to be. She had no idea what happened to Ed after that, but in the years to come she sometimes realized she was looking for his prototype; in fact, she started going out with Owen because he vaguely reminded her of that long-ago love.

"Tell me about the girl," Lydia said. "What was she like?"

"Like the papers said. Shy. Quiet. Reserved."

He put his head down for a minute on his knees. When he lifted it, the words came with a rush. "You want the truth? She spooked me out. Fifteen years old, did I say? That's what I thought she was at first. This small high voice and the cute dresses and something about that rabbity look on the little-girl face. Then talking to her, I found she'd been out of high school two years, she was nineteen. Well, nineteen years old.

Sometimes you have to live with your parents, you can't afford anything else. But you figure it's just temporary. You're marking time till something breaks. It's nothing to do with whether you get along with your parents or not. You just want out—that's natural. It's the way it happened with me. When I got a job in North Rainey and moved out of Pendil Park, my parents understood. No hard feelings. But there's that girl planning on staying around. Planning it, like she said, for keeps. She wants to go in for some serious decorating job in a house that belongs to her old man. I mean, something weird about it."

Lydia checked her notes. "It says in the other detective's report you once drove her home. That means the D.A.'s office knows about it too and are going to make hay of it. So what do they know? Who in the store saw her? Where did she sit? Jerry, exactly what happened?"

"Well." He seemed more tense. "She just came in, she said the wall is all smooth, she's ready for the next step, what do I have in mind. So I told her what she needed, a couple of gallons of primer, we could deliver them the next day. Next day? Morning or afternoon? I said all our deliveries were afternoon. So then she shook her head. That would mean she'd be wasting the whole morning, she'd just take the cans and carry them herself. Four blocks to the bus and three when she got off. And she put on that martyr look. You know? Well, it was almost five-thirty, and I was going in her direction anyhow, so I said if she'd wait twenty minutes, I'd drive her."

"You suggested it?"

The open face darkened. "I suppose you could say so. But the way she stood there, picking up a gallon in each hand, showing me how strong and brave she was. And besides, I was flattered. Annoyed but flattered too—okay, I admit it. I mean, if a girl keeps asking for you. Anyhow, it was a damn fool thing to do. I was sorry the moment she set foot in the car."

"What'd you talk about?"

"Paint," his fierce voice said. "Yellow paint, only sometimes she called it ocher. And what'd I think about a stencil around the top of the wall. She was working on designs. You could buy them ready-made in kits, there was this Victorian daisy thing she liked, but she thought maybe she'd make her own. I told her I didn't know anything about that stuff, so she went back to paint. Was yellow the right color? What did yellow look like when the sun came in between one and four? That's when I found out she was home between one and four. Home the whole day, sounded like. I tell you, she was a weirdo. She's dead now, I don't want to say anything bad about her, but a nineteen-year-old girl staying home all day, that can really spook you out."

"How about when you got to her house?"

"I picked up the cans and carried them to the front door, and she said did I want to see the job she'd done. Well. I didn't especially want to, but you can't be rude. So I carried them upstairs."

"Anyone around? Mother? Father? Sisters?"

"Not then. Her father came home later." His face tightened under the fair eyebrows. "She showed me the job she'd done, the four walls all smooth, she said something like I should be proud. I helped her, I was really responsible.''

''What'd you think?''

''Listen. That room. It was fit for a five-year-old,'' he said earnestly. ''Some pictures of, I don't know, shepherdesses on the wall, and these dolls all around, and a lamp shaped like some animal. A rabbit, I swear. A bunny rabbit with a music box. She said would I like her to turn it on, and I said not especially, but she did anyhow, and this tinny music comes out while the rabbit goes up and down, up and down, poking at a wooden carrot. Gross, know what I mean?''

Lydia did know. Addie had a lamp like that, though hers was not a rabbit but a boy and girl on a seesaw. You wound it up and the seesaw moved in jerky syncopation to the tinkly tune. Owen gave it to her. Cute, isn't it, he'd said. Cute, but like so much of what he did, unsuitable, Addie being then not quite two. Lydia decided not to point out that a two-year-old knocks things over, bangs into them, can easily crash light bulbs on the floor—she put the lamp in the closet and takes it out on the rare occasions when Owen comes to pick up the child.

She nodded at Jerry. ''Anything special go on when you were up there with her?''

''I told you. She turned on that drippy music. That's when her father came home. Anyhow, a door banged downstairs and she said, 'That's my dad.'''

''Did you see him?''

''No. He must've been in the kitchen when I went out.''

"Anything happen between you and her?"

"What's that supposed to mean?"

"Jerry, you're alone with a girl in her bedroom. You don't know her father is coming home. Did you kiss her? Put an arm around her? These are questions the prosecution is going to ask. If I don't ask them I'm not being fair to you."

He glowered above her desk. "Listen. I didn't kiss her, I didn't put an arm around her. If you want to know, I couldn't wait to get out of there. Like I said, she spooked me out. You don't have to believe it, but that's the truth."

She wants to believe it. Or, rather, she does believe it, all the telling and ill-flavored details: the little-girl bravery, and the flattering insistence on using him, and the decorating scheme "for keeps," and the distaste of a virile young man for all that inapt juvenilia. Her client has relayed them, and she believes him. The only thing is, there is still that ending to account for: a young girl in a corner of a parking lot with her features smashed, her body violated. Beginning and end: an anomaly. Nothing fits.

She was the one to walk around now. She said there were a few more items to get clear at this first meeting. She understands he has an alibi. She wants to hear about it from him, and she'll also want to talk to the girl—what's her name? Yes. Fern Eaton. And she'll go to see the place where the crime took place, and she wants a list of people she can count on for references. It's a job that normally would take two months, and because she was late getting into this she has to conclude it in two weeks. Which makes it doubly important that she get cooperation from him.

His pleasant face was as businesslike as hers. Okay, his alibi. What exactly does she want to know? He went to see Fern that night around eight. They talked about going out, but his car was on the blink, and the restaurant they usually went to was almost a mile away. Too far to walk. And she said there was some food around, so why didn't they just stay home. Which they did. Did anyone see them? No. Did anyone call and perhaps he answered the phone? No. Did Fern's roommate happen to come home while he was there? Not that either. But he was there, all right, and Fern would bear him out.

"Is she a serious girl friend, Jerry?"

"I haven't seen anyone much since this business started. I just—I can't put my heart in it. After work I want to go home and sleep."

"Well, were you serious before? Did you look on it as a possibly permanent arrangement?"

"Would it look better if I did?"

She banged her fist down on the desk. "Look here. I thought we got all that straight. Whatever there was or is in your life, the prosecution is going to find out about it. They probably know already, they've had more time at this than I have. And it's going to come out at the trial. So you have your choice. Do you want them to surprise you with the facts, or do you want to tell me everything and let me put it in the best possible light?"

He sighed. Okay. Fern was an okay girl and she'd like it to be, as Miss Ness said, serious, but he wasn't ready to settle down. Maybe he'd stay at the hardware store the rest of his life. Maybe not. He wants to be free to decide. No strings. No responsibilities. That's why he dated other girls once in a while. Not steady like Fern, but cute girls, he likes to kid around with them.

"And another thing," his earnest voice said. "I can . . . I mean, I can have . . ."

"You mean sex?" For a second, he was a young man and that inappropriate gender was again in the way.

"Yes. All right. I can go to bed with Fern any time I want. I'm not bragging. You just said to tell you everything, and that's part of it. I mean, why would I want to—well, why would I have anything to do with a girl like Pam when I'm not hard up in that department?"

It was there again: boyish candor, supple arrogance. She wrote down Fern, cute girls, kid around, sex. More telling details, though she would have to think carefully how to use the argument implicit in them.

Now references, she said. Who would he suggest?

He was ready. Old Man Neils, of course. And Chipper Collins, he was the oldest salesman, had been there twenty years. And his landlady, a Mrs. Forbes, he sometimes does maintenance for her. Plumbing, carpentry, stuff like that, he knows she appreciates it. Is that enough?

Might be too much, she thought. In her old practice, a judge would not have let it all in. But Ben said this was different: a community, with relaxed rules of admissibility. Let folks talk about each other.

"How about high school? You've been out"—she glanced at her notes—"four years? They'd surely remember you."

"Mr. Ahearn, the principal, he's a decent guy, he'd give me a good sendoff— No, don't ask him. No reason. On second thought, just don't."

"Is there someone close to your family? Some old family friend who's known you since boyhood, maybe?"

"My parents did have this friend. Felix Chubb, his name is. Lots older than they are, he's sort of my godfather. But no, not him either. His wife died a couple of years ago and he went into this nursing home on the Island and they don't let him out. Listen. With Fern and the store and the landlady, didn't I give you plenty?"

Felix Chubb, godfather, she wrote, and crossed it out. It was true; he gave her plenty. He answered all the questions she asked and some she didn't. And always the open face radiating the same expression: quizzical pride, earnest frankness, the desire to please. She looked carefully, but she could detect no underlying layer of calculation or slyness. A jury wouldn't detect it either. Defensiveness and anger, yes, but not slyness; he would be an admirable witness.

But still, shaking hands with him, making plans for their next meeting, she had a sense, not of anything actually withheld, but of remote corners, deep places—an anomalous component that would require a monumental combination of luck and guile if she were to stumble in on it.

THREE

"LYDIA, what's this I read in the papers."

It was the way Owen talked. What's this they're giving us for dessert. What's this I hear about a rent increase. What's this about Addie having an allergy. Lydia moved the phone to the other ear. "Hello, Owen."

"So tell me all."

"I don't know why anyone had to write about it." There had been a paragraph in the gossip column of an evening newspaper: "Jerry Eldstrom has switched lawyers. His new one is Lydia Ness of the Benjamin H. Lyttle office. Can it be he thinks a woman is a better bet for wooing the jury in a rape case?" She wanted to think the deposed lawyer, out of pique or perhaps relief, had given the news, but also she couldn't repress the idea that Ben, out of his insatiable desire for publicity, had himself engineered the leak.

"I was surprised to read it," Owen said.

"I guess I was surprised to be doing it." She could see this would be a long conversation; she sat down.

"I remember you once saying you'd be tarred and feathered before you defended a rapist."

That's the thing about ex-husbands. Time diminishes them, distance diminishes them, a purposeful detachment diminishes them, and yet out of the mass of undifferentiated years they can zero in on the one salient moment. They have your number. "Possibly they've got the wrong man."

"That contingency is always possible, isn't it?"

Enough of this conversation. "Owen, how's Marcy?" she asked.

"Doing good. One of the partners has been sick, and last week they sent Marcy to look at a couple of locations."

Marcy was Owen's second wife. She worked as a secretary to a firm that found locations for TV commercials. "Owen, that's great."

"A breakfast room she picked out is actually going to be in an ad for cereal next month."

"I'll switch to that cereal."

"Just shows what good judgment she has. That's why I thought you'd want to know. That she agrees with me about this."

"About what?"

"That you're asking for trouble. Messing with people like that."

"Owen, what are you talking about?" She kicked off her shoes; a longer talk even than she'd thought.

"I know those people. Marcy and I, we both do. The girl's family, I mean. Not a nickel in the bank, but lots of family feeling. Maybe too much family feeling. Let one be hurt and they're all hurt, they're out for blood. They don't care if it's the correct blood or not—just that they want it. So you should stay away from them."

"Owen, I'm not fighting that girl's family. In fact, I feel for them, how could I not? All I'm doing is making a case for a young man so a jury can decide if he is or isn't guilty.''

''That's what you think,'' he said.

Part of her was annoyed. When things were difficult enough, what right did he have to upset her, interject his own muddled ideas. But also she had to smile. It was typical: in his wrong-headed way, Owen trying to be solicitous, attempting helpfulness in circumstances about which he had no real understanding. In fact, if anyone knew from experience about the economic status of the victim's family, it was she. When she and Owen were married, the year she got out of college, she had no money and was in debt for four years of tuition besides. Owen, on the other hand, turned out to have enough money to start a limousine service. It was Lydia's suspicion, after she got to know Owen better, that his father had provided that money so his bumbling son would not come into his own business, which was manufacturing office furniture. Whatever the case, the limousines made it right away; Owen was the first to say that he succeeded not through any special brains or talent on his part but by being in the right place at the right time. Indeed, if financial success was the measure, the first years of their marriage hit it off all around. Owen tripled his fleet and put his drivers in purple uniforms, and Lydia brought home a respectable salary as office manager of an import-export firm. ''Manager'' was an understatement; when her boss started taking off first one and then two-and-a-half and then three days a week, she understood that he understood she was running the show. ''I'm going to ask him for more money," she said to Owen one night. "Do you want it?" he asked. "I earn it, don't I?" "I mean, do you want to work there?" When she told him the truth, which was that she was bored silly, he looked thoughtful. She'd always said she wanted to go to law school, he pointed out. "Owen, I wouldn't be bringing in a penny for three years." "We can swing it, honey. If we're careful. I didn't want that country house anyhow."

As he was to say later, it was his greatest mistake. But that verdict wasn't offered for six years, during which time she completed law school and, the limousine fleet having tripled again, felt free to take the job she wanted, which was at Legal Aid, and presently confronted her clients with not just a woman attorney but a pregnant woman attorney. It wasn't till after Addie was born that Owen came to her with his big declaration. Having staked her to a law career, he had done himself a great disservice, was what he said. Now that she was an LLD, she was too brainy for him. Things had been ducky when she worked for that import-export company, but now he no longer felt comfortable with her. They didn't read the same books or listen to the same music or like the same movies—even their taste in food was different. Also, now he was letting it all out, he had to admit there was someone else. A cute girl called Marcy Burns. He wanted to marry her.

He made this surprising announcement when Addie was four weeks old. Lydia had been holding the baby, trying to elicit a precocious smile, but she put her down and looked at Owen dumbfounded. He'd been so assiduous during her pregnancy. The exercise classes, the deep breathing, the doctor's visits, the special menus. The little gifts, the encouragement during those last cumbersome weeks, the supportive presence at delivery. Owen, the model husband—how in four weeks could he have changed?

It was not four weeks, he said. He'd been in love with Marcy for a year. But just when he'd been gearing himself to tell Lydia, she had announced that she was pregnant. "I didn't think it was fair to walk out on you then," he said.

She thought of the time she suddenly had to throw up, and he stopped the car and held her shoulders while she heaved by the side of the road. Or the week during the third month when they thought she might miscarry, and he insisted on bringing food and bed pans while she stayed in bed. Or the moments when he would put a rapturous ear to her rumbling stomach and sing to that unborn child a nursery rhyme. "Owen, do you really mean that all those months, when we were going to classes together, reading the books on child care, buying baby furniture, all that time..."

"I thought you shouldn't be alone," he said simply.

That was Owen. Kindly but wrong-headed. Sweet but muddled. Not, as he said, brainy, but possessed of an implacable stubbornness once he got an idea in his head. She couldn't get over it. That all that show of devotion, the concerned interest, the tremulous expectation, had been false. Lydia looked up at the wall where there was a pretty poster illustrating a child's book. Owen had it hanging over the crib the day they came back from the hospital. "Let her learn to appreciate good art right away," he'd said. Lydia kept her gaze on the pink fluff of clouds; she had never been so angry in her life. She was so angry that she thought it would impair her feelings for the baby; how could she love anything whose coming had so demeaned her, made her the object of such duplicity and misguided sacrifice?

That deluded idea, that her feeling for the baby might be impaired, lasted less than twenty-four hours. Sometimes, picking up the child, she would think, How could I have been so dumb, to suppose that anything could spoil it. Me and this baby. Me and this cuddly luscious beautiful baby.

Addie is less cuddly now. Or, rather, at three years old, she mandates cuddling at times and places of her own choosing. But it's still me and her. Lydia and Addie. A connectedness that is palpable and intense and mysterious; she can no more understand how it works than she understands how a telephone works, or television. Black magic, she says dismissively when Douglas in his pedagogic way tries to fill her in on the eminently fundamental facts about electrodes and electrical impulses to explain how it is that a figure in a studio can be relayed in all its color and shape and mobility onto a screen a hundred miles away, and in the same way she finds magic in the sensitivity that causes Addie to respond to what seem entirely silent signals from her mother. Last night was typical. Everything went right. Bubbles in the bath and three chapters of a favorite book and the lamb chop supper

Addie likes best and some feats of imaginative splendor when the two of them were playing house. "But I don't know," she said to Diane at nursery school this morning. "Something's wrong. She woke at one o'clock with a nightmare."

Except, of course, she does know. It's Addie demonstrating that mysterious affinity in which the secret dismay of a mother can exercise its subtle imbalance over the psyche of a child. She moved the phone to her other ear. Of course Owen had it wrong, but in his bumbling way he had also got it right. Her heart twists at the thought of having to meet the vengeful and devastated gaze of those who have lost their saint, their paragon, their exemplar of sweetness, their beloved sister/daughter.

She heard her voice modulate into the animated tone she tries to put on for Owen. She has long since gotten over her anger at him. In a pragmatic way, they worked out the financial arrangements; he will pay for Addie's education, including the expensive all-day nursery school she goes to now, but for nothing else—this seems to Lydia fair in view of her own salary and also the support he gave her years ago. And she truly wishes him and Marcy well; when their conversations aren't about Addie, they're about the large and excessively possessive family that marriage with Marcy has landed him in. Uncle Max, who is in the wine business and who insists on his visits that they sample each of the dozen bottles he has brought; cousin Lois, whose mobiles with their precipitous copper cascades Marcy hangs in the living room; the twin sister Louann, whose weekly visits would be acceptable did they not include the boyfriend Marcy knows perfectly well that Owen can't stand; and now Uncle Charlie.

"He did what, Owen?" she asked absently.

"Solid black. The whole bathroom. Lyddy, I just told you. His way of saying thank you because we let him use the apartment when we went away for a week. And I like to walk around in the morning—well, Lyddy, you know how I like to walk around in the morning. It's healthy being nude, good for the pores, but I don't know, a black bathroom, somehow it changes everything."

"Can't you paint it over?"

"Marcy says no. After all the trouble he took, at it for three whole days, she says it would hurt his feelings."

"Poor Owen." Mentally she patted his hand. Among the matters to which Owen wasn't sensitive was the attitude suitable for a divorced couple: cloaked hostility balanced by an edgy friendliness on those occasions when their mutual child was present. She knew half a dozen divorced couples, and this was the posture into which their relationship naturally fell. On the other hand, the relationship between her and Owen was structured on his belief that since she knew him better than anyone else, she was better qualified than anyone else to offer him counseling; on marrying Marcy, he had simply moved Lydia, in his mind, from the category of loving wife to what might be defined as caring and knowledgeable sister—he had started calling with his plaintive queries on the day he and Marcy came back from their honeymoon.

Yes, she said now, everything going fine at nursery school. No, that teacher he talked to when he once picked up Addie (it was four months ago, she thought), that woman is gone, but there's another, Diane, she seems most tuned in. Where is Addie now? He'd like to talk to her. Oh, sorry, she's gone upstairs for a few minutes to the Barlows'. Janey Barlow has a new doll house she wanted Addie to see. Yes, Pat Barlow, that tall, skinny, owlish woman he met once in the elevator, she's the mother. Yes, it is a boon to have another family like that in the apartment house.

Then he cleared his throat. "Incidentally..." he said. She smiled. Such a transparent man. "Incidentally" at the end of a conversation, which means that now he has got to the important part, what all along he's been working up to say. "Incidentally, Marcy decided she wanted to go to her high school reunion, a picnic in this town in Westchester where she went to school, so we won't be able to take Addie next weekend. Lydia, I hope it doesn't put you to any inconvenience."

Lydia dropped the phone and then picked it up. Usually she doesn't mind that Owen lets months slip by without claiming his right to have Addie every other weekend—in fact, she prefers it. Though she knows the basics are attended to when Addie goes off with him and Marcy, the child invariably comes home afflicted with a certain desuetude and armed with some unsuitable gifts: a furtrimmed jacket, an antique doll dressed in lace and satin, a microscope, a puzzle of five hundred pieces. Or Addie reports that the show made her yawn so much they had to leave in the middle and Lydia gradually discerns that Owen has expected his three-year-old daughter to appreciate the raucous singing and dazzling dancing of a musical comedy. It's as if, having gone in for all that misapplied fervor and meretricious attention for nine months, Owen is unable to keep track of the years that follow; in his mind the child may be three, but she may also be five or seven or thirteen.

But today! Letting her down at the last minute this week! Oh, Owen, it's not inconvenient, it's just killing, is all it is. Did it ever occur to you what I have to do in the next fourteen days? Interview every witness, and coach every witness so their story comes out the way I want it, and write my opening statement, and figure out the questions for cross-examination...

"Lyddy, I wish we weren't going. School reunions, I hate those things, you know that," his protesting voice went on. "Everyone there has turned into an orthopedic surgeon or a great trombone player or something important in the State Department, and they ask what I do, and I say a limousine service, and they say how interesting, how really interesting. And Marcy kisses everyone, even the ones she tells me in advance she hated, they made her life miserable when she was seventeen."

Lydia laughed. She could never stay angry at Owen long; that had been the fact three years ago and it was still the fact today. His thinking was too muddled, his protests too profuse and disingenuous; in whatever his misdeeds consisted, they were as likely to work into trouble for himself as for anyone else. Besides, a foretaste of the next couple of weeks suddenly went through her. When Owen murmured that they weren't leaving till noon Saturday, he could take Addie for a few hours in the morning if that would be a help, she said no. She could manage. She'd get a sitter. Or Pat Barlow would help out. Or she'd arrange her work so she could be with Addie herself. A shudder went through her very bones, and she thought she was going to want Addie where she could see her, touch her, feel her every minute.

FOUR

LATER, LYDIA THOUGHT HOW unnecessary it had been to go to the parking lot at all. Granted that you're supposed to familiarize yourself with the scene of the crime, but this crime had taken place three months before; it was not a matter of her eagle eyes discerning any secret clues or finding any mitigating factors. Here is where the girl had been found, here is where, indubitably, the deed had been done. Furthermore, the place had been thoroughly scrutinized by the police and pictured in the newspapers: every broken link in the fence, every puddle of oil on the rough cement, every pile of sodden leaves, cigarette butts, and wrinkled candy wrappers. One paper had even shown it as it appeared at different times of day: at nine in the morning, when the students streamed across its barren length; at four, when the sun glared down on its treeless expanse and a few boys came to shoot baskets or toss a ball on the field in back; and also of course at night, unlit, untenanted, as presumably it had been at that fatal hour. So why did she come? Was it just an exercise in morbidity? Why didn't she realize that in a place like North Rainey this exposure was bound to lead to trouble?

Besides, she had been busy—standing here, where the gritty surface was all that was left of that mountain of sand, she was appalled to think of all she had packed into the past two days. First a visit to Jerry's girl friend, Fern, who pushed up the sleeves of her pink sweater and swore in her husky voice that Jerry had been with her on the night in question. A Tuesday. She was the receptionist at a health club that was open Wednesday and Monday nights, so Tuesday nights were what you might call sacred. Usually they go out for dinner, a cute Spanish restaurant, well, not really Spanish but they call it that because of the pictures of bullfighting on the walls—that's their favorite. But Jerry said his car was on the blink, and they both were tired, so they decided not to walk the eighteen blocks. Especially since there was this casserole she and her roommate had cooked up over the weekend. And they decided not to go to the movies, either, another of those films about high school kids, how much of those immature darlings can a person stand? And she'll swear to this in court. Also to the fact that Jerry didn't do it. Jerry Eldstrom kill someone! Rape her! Bizarre. A sweet, friendly, gentle type like Jerry. Oh, he gets a little sulky sometimes, but what guy wouldn't, on his feet all day and the customers bitching about this and that, but anything really mean— never. Besides, why would he go in for rape when he can... well, maybe she shouldn't be saying this, but Miss Ness said to be honest, and the fact is she personally would never deny Jerry any pleasure and she's not ashamed to say so.

She put her arms behind her neck, revealing small rounded breasts—the kind of figure a health club would be glad to have for display at their front desk. It would be displayed to advantage to the jury also—

that and the argument implicit in it that a man to whom such a treasure was available would not be likely to go skulking about in the dark reaches of a parking lot for his thrills.

Profile of a non-rapist: much the same argument emerged from Jerry's boss and colleagues, along with the tributes to probity, good humor, industriousness, virtue. "Women like him," said Chipper Collins, who at fifty-four had been working at Neils' longer than any other salesman. "Don't ask me why. He's not particularly good looking, well, not to my way of thinking, maybe someone of your sex sees it different. But there it is. Say there are three of us behind the counter, a woman comes in, she'll go to Jerry. At first it pissed me off. Young upstart like that, what right did he have to be singled out? Then I realized he didn't do anything. Just stood there with that little half smile on his face that tells them no matter how dumb their questions, he'll have patience. And it works. Time and again, I see it working. This woman who's in a state comes in and right away she's telling Jerry how her ceiling is peeling a week after the painter did it and swore she'd never again have trouble, you can't depend on anyone. And Jerry listens and promises nothing, and they go out feeling better."

As for Mr. Neils, he sat at his desk in the small office in back that afforded no privacy and said Jerry was good for business. "The customers like him, they like to stand talking to him. He thinks it's because he's such a whiz at construction. Don't tell him I told you so, but he doesn't know beans about construction. Reading a few how-to books, that's nothing. If you snip off a piece of your little finger when you're using the circular saw, if your measurements are off by half an inch and you have to shell out your own money for getting the job redone...that's how you learn about construction. Besides, he's still young, Jerry is. Don't tell him I said so, but he gets carried away. Last month he heard about this new tar for sealing roofs. It could be applied in the rain, that was the special gimmick. It didn't work, that was the bottom line. So what do you do with the three hundred gallons of unsalable tar your best salesman has ordered? You give it away, that's what. A half-dozen mistakes like that, you can lose your shirt. But he'll learn. Don't tell him I said so, but he has plenty of time to learn. He says he's in the business to stay and I believe him. This is what he likes, relating to people. People: read 'women.' When I started in this business, a woman shrieked if she had to change a fuse. Now they count for a good half of our business. My neighbor, a skinny little thing, weighs less than a hundred, I bet, she dug a ditch all around her house and then lined it with cement to stop water seeping into the cellar. Another one down the block is shingling the whole front of her house. She alone, up on a ladder. Drive down Willow right this minute, I bet you'll see her. That's how this trouble started. That damn girl comes in, she wants to take off wallpaper. Twenty years ago she'd have called a man to take off wallpaper. I wish to God she had. I wish we never saw her. But Jerry didn't force himself on her, not Jerry Eldstrom, I'll never believe it.''

And finally Jerry's landlady, a Mrs. Hannah Forbes, whom Lydia had visited this morning. Like the others, she wasn't loath to talk. Tell Lydia about Jerry? About Jerry Eldstrom? About the absolutely crazy mistake they're making, she's never heard anything so wild in her life? Well, sure. What does Miss Ness want to know?

She'd been cleaning, her gray hair was tied in a scarf and she had something on the stove, but after a few preliminaries, she sat with Lydia in the living room, which was too crowded with furniture. "Sit there," she said. "Careful! Don't fall on that footstool— good. In here is stuff from three rooms. What can you do when your husband dies and the kids grow up? You put everything in one room and rent the top floor, that's what. And I never rented to anyone nicer than Jerry. So now what can I tell you besides that he's considerate and polite and always pleasant and he didn't do it?"

Lydia mentioned that Jerry had told her he helped with the maintenance.

"Oh, that. I don't give him anything for it, he just wants to be helpful. It's really a sweet thing the way he wants to be helpful. One time there was a leak under the kitchen sink, water going down into the basement. He said don't call the plumber, they charge an arm and a leg, he'll fix it himself. So he works all one Sunday morning, and after three hours he says I can relax, the job is done. And on Monday after he leaves for work it's leaking worse than ever. When the plumber came, he said a couple more hours, we'd have a real flood. But don't let on to Jerry. After all he did, I wouldn't want him to feel bad."

Mrs. Forbes maneuvered around a desk and two chairs to get into the kitchen. When she came back, she said there was another thing. ''Once when my fifteen-year-old granddaughter was visiting, I went to the hospital for some tests and they made me stay overnight. So there was the girl all alone. But I told her she didn't have to worry because Jerry was upstairs, with him in the house she'd be safe. And Jerry was in the house, and she was safe. Now I ask you. My own grandchild, would I have said that if I didn't think that Jerry Eldstrom...'' She put out her hands as if searching for the adequate words. Then she said was there anything else. She doesn't much like to leave her house these days, but she'll come on the double if Lydia wants her at the trial.

Lydia did want her. Her and all the others—she thought about them as she stood at the place where a girl had not been safe. She was hot; second week of June, and this was the third time the temperature had hit ninety. She was also tired. She had not just heard the testimonials. She had rehearsed with their eager expositors the questions that would be asked, coached them on suitable attire, whittled down the exuberant replies, advised on courtroom procedure. Now she looked up and down the lot. A man was sweeping down near the school and some boys were getting their bikes out of the bicycle rack and, outside the fence, a car was slowing down, but where she stood, nothing of interest. Only on the ground a few crumpled pages from a notebook, some leaves from the maples outside, a couple of those oil puddles the newspapers had made a point of capturing. Once when she was a young girl her father took the family to a battlefield where one of the fiercest Civil War battles had been fought. "Can't you just imagine it?" he'd said, his voice shaking with emotion. "The dead horses, the stench, the gaping wounds, the cries of those maimed survivors." She couldn't. She tried to imagine, she really did try, but nothing in the stubbled fields and jutting rocks and few trees could evoke for her a sense of that terrible carnage, and in the same way there was nothing in this desolate corner to make a rape come alive. She tried reconstructing it. Here's where he parked the car, on this portion of cracked cement he dragged her out, in this corner is where he pushed her down...Useless. Then she understood. She was trying to attach those ugly movements to Jerry. To that affable, polite, sweet-tempered fellow who couldn't fix a leak or judge a roofing tar, and whose ineptitude along these lines those who liked him took such pains to cover up.

She took out her camera. Maybe if she takes the pictures herself and studies them at night, the scene will come alive. This is no time for visualizing rape: four o'clock in the afternoon in a town where she can still taste on her lips the seafood salad she had for lunch at a pleasant restaurant two blocks away. She focused the camera; at the same time she realized that two women had got out of their car and were heading for her.

"You a reporter?" The shorter woman didn't bother with a greeting.

Lydia said she wasn't.

"You writing a book?"

Not that either.

"You just like to take pictures of places where someone was killed?" No greeting and no introductions, either. She didn't need them. Something about the accusatory gaze, the bloated look, as if under that smooth skin, rage was biding its time. Besides, there was a family resemblance. If these weren't the faces she had seen in the newspaper, leading those stricken children into the funeral parlor, they looked like them. The same saucer-shaped eyes, flat foreheads, slightly too diminutive mouths with the heavily indented upper lip. She decided to meet it head on. "I'm the lawyer," she said.

"*His* lawyer, Maureen," the taller sister murmured, as though an explanation were needed. When nothing more was said, she understood they were sizing her up. Not the appraisal a neutral stranger might give, appreciating the good points, deprecating the bad. Out of those cold round eyes came an inimical assessment, as if by studying her suit, her features, her hairdo, they could divine how to get the better of her.

"You should be ashamed." Maureen spoke with explosive force. She was wearing a sundress with a short red jacket, and the red lapels shook as she bit off the words.

"Listen. It's ghastly about what happened to your sister. That is, it is your sister, isn't it?" Lydia said.

"You should be ashamed." Maureen again.

When Lydia backed away a step or two, she felt her heel go into something sticky on the cement. "I just think everyone's entitled to that day in court," she said.

"Not a rapist. Not a man who would do that."
Their eyes with that inculpatory glare again surveyed
the area, and she understood. The scene that had been
impossible for her to conjure up was quivering before
their eyes. Every detail inscribed in their fevered imag-
inations. "I guess you mean Jerry Eldstrom."

"Don't say that name in my presence," Maureen
wailed.

Lydia shifted her pocketbook from one shoulder to
the other. She had imagined this confrontation as
taking place in the courtroom. At its worst, even if the
family sat in the front row, there would be a distance
of ten or twelve feet to shield her. That and the cere-
monial decorum of the room itself, the dignity that
attaches to counsel, the presence of other participants. In her most dread imaginings it had never occurred to her that there would be a meeting in which
they were standing shoulder to shoulder, so close that
she could reach out to touch Maureen's red and white
shoulder straps, the pale blue dress of the other sister.

"She was the sweetest girl. The family was everything to her. She could relate to everyone in some
special way. Every sister and brother, every in-law,
every child. No matter what happened in your life, you
knew Pam would say the right thing about it. Or not
say anything, if that's what you needed. She had an
instinct." The taller sister had a low, level voice, she
didn't bite off the words like Maureen. She was the
dental hygienist, Lydia decided. You could hear her,
in her even tones, saying, Looks like those back lower
molars aren't getting the attention they need.

"It's terrible," Lydia murmured. "Terrible."

"My mother had a stroke after it happened. We don't call it that, we're trying not to alarm her, but she has trouble raising her right arm and her speech is slurred. The shock was just too much. For years Pam's been cooking for her. She made this special custard my mother loved, you have to be careful putting in the yolk or it curdles. Only Pam could do it right."

Lydia shook her head.

"And my father—God knows why he isn't in the hospital right now. He gets these awful headaches. Pam used to massage his head. It was the only way he got relief. She had this magic touch, he said. Only Pam."

"Even the children." Maureen, back in the act. "If we're going away for even a night, my two won't let anyone stay with them unless it's Aunt Pam. Same with your kids, Amy. Right?" Maureen looked out toward the car, and Lydia could see four or five children peering out. "And you want that man to get off."

"Oh, listen. All I want is for the jury to have a reasonable crack at deciding if he's innocent or guilty."

"Suppose it was your daughter." Maureen had followed her glance, and for a second Lydia's heart twisted. Then she realized. They don't know anything. It's just the standard crude taunt that flourishes in moments of fury. Wait till it's your mother who gets mugged. Would you like your sister to marry one?

"I know you lawyers with your fancy tricks," Maureen said.

"Fancy tricks. Oh, no," Lydia murmured.

"Otherwise, why did he change lawyers?" Maureen came closer, as if proximity could enhance the snapping words. "He figured someone from your hotshot office could railroad him through."

"Actually, he wasn't the one to request the change; his parents did it."

"Curses on his parents," Maureen said.

"I spit on his parents," Amy said in the measured tones that turned out to be as capable of embodying rage as her sister's.

Lydia moved back another inch. Owen was right after all about what they wanted. Jerry's head on a platter. Innocent or guilty, Jerry Eldstrom's head on a platter.

She could still feel them appraising her. Standing in this place where she couldn't visualize the crime and they could visualize nothing else, they were staring at her as if she were—what? Subhuman? Beneath contempt? She knew what it was to smart under the fury of others, of course she did. How can you work as a defense lawyer and not at one time or another be on the receiving end of scorn, bitterness, hostility, rage? But it's courtroom rage; it's confined to a certain time and place, it attaches to a particular set of circumstances. However savagely you and the district attorney duel, you know that if you meet someplace else, the elevator, say, the steps outside, the two of you can summon up an exchange that is civil, even humorous.

This was different. The feeling emanating from these two had the wild illogic and free-wheeling viciousness of people in a feud. She had sometimes wondered about those feuds; they played so big a part in folklore that they must be authentic, but how could they be? How could it happen that two reasonable and intelligent people who had never set eyes on each other before were destined to be gripped by a murderous enmity because of something that had occurred two, maybe three generations earlier? Now she understood. Or, rather, she understood what it was to be the recipient of such enmity. In the minds of these women, she was tainted. Besmirched. Enrolled in Jerry Eldstrom's guilt. Nothing she could do would change it. No gesture she could make would mollify it. It was a case of one side or the other: if you're not with us, you're against us. She could say a hundred times that she was sorry, such a terrible crime, her heart went out to them, and in their ears the words would come out a travesty.

She looked across the playground, where the bicycle rack was now empty. So much enmity dishonors you. Justified or not, it's too overpowering for you to carry. One part of her yearned for release. To get out from under that hot, heavy anger. The office had hired her a car and driver, and she wished that Willis, the driver, who was now waiting behind the sisters' car under the plunging branches of an old maple, would call to her, fabricate some reason why she must immediately come. At the same time, she knew this was a dream opportunity. To speak to the family and friends of those on the other side is a right to which theoretically the defense attorney is entitled, but one which in this case the family would have no qualms about refusing. If Jerry Eldstrom's attorney walked up to Pam Howells's house and said she wanted to have a chat, the door would doubtless be slammed in her face. But here the sisters are, in a bind that they themselves have made.

"Something I wonder," she said. "How can you be so sure it was Jerry who did it?"

"She said his name on the phone. Jerry."

"Couldn't it have been someone else? Someone she'd talked to about that nice, helpful clerk at the hardware store?"

"She had no men friends. She never went out. Who would she have told?"

"Or maybe another clerk, taking advantage—Oh, look. Don't jump right away. I'm just trying to get the truth of it."

"The truth is that none of the other clerks have an old green car. The police went into it," Amy said coldly.

"But Jerry didn't use his car, it was parked all night on the street."

"And you expect us to believe that?" But there was less force in the woman's voice; the weight of all that enmity must be wearing them down too.

"Did anyone go out on the porch or try to see the man?" she asked.

"I wish to God I had. I wanted to tell her it wasn't right, a young man ought to come in, meet the family, show himself." Amy, and all at once the words weren't measured at all. Ah. So the shadow of her negligence lies along that bright dazzle of pain.

Lydia looked out past the fence. The children in the car were getting restless. She could faintly hear them:

"Hey, quit it." "You quit it yourself." They must be stifling in that car. But they were well-brought-up children. Either that or intimidated; they wouldn't interrupt. "You mean you were there that night?"

The mouth with its deeply indented upper lip moved in fierce contortions.

"Stacy and me," she said finally.

"Why didn't you tell her?"

"She seemed so happy. Her eyes shone. We told her to change her scarf, and when she put it on I could see her hands were shaking. Oh, God, I'll never forgive myself."

"Amy, cut it out." Maureen put a hand on the other's arm; it was a scene that had been played before, Lydia saw.

"So no one actually watched her get into a car."

"I saw her go down the front walk. She went slowly, those small, deliberate steps, that was her style. Then on the street she turned toward the left. Cars were parked in front of the house, it's a busy street these days since they changed the bus routes, lots of times you can't even get into your own driveway. I figured he was partway down the block."

Lydia thought of that house. She had had Willis drive her by it this morning. The brown clapboard, the unadorned porch with its two brown rockers, the small apron of lawn in front containing nothing but a couple of barberries, a spindly rhododendron.

"She was going to fix up the front lawn," Amy said, as if reading her thoughts. "She was studying gardening books. She had all these plans, she was going to start planting this fall. My parents were longing for some flowers, maybe a few nice bushes, but my mother couldn't do anything like digging with her arthritis. And my father, that tricky heart, he's not supposed to try anything heavy. So Pam said she'd do it.''

The standard denouement: for Pam to do it. The gardening, the baby-sitting, the cooking, the nursing. Lots of families have one like that. Occasionally a boy, but more often a girl. One sacrificial lamb to stay on with the old folks, cosset them, make a nest for them when their bad backs and fragile hearts and arthritic fingers no longer permit them to work at it themselves. As the girl goes without perceptible break from docile virgin to elderly spinster, the others recite the myth of her willingness. She loves to cook. She's so happy pottering around the house. She adores staying with our children. No one else knows how to stroke his forehead. And of course the correlative that justifies it all, makes it valid: she's so shy, withdrawn, she just doesn't seem to want to go out. They all lead their full energetic lives satisfied in the assurance that Ma and Pa are not alone in their infirmity; the glass ornaments are being dusted, the mahogany table polished, the custard made without curdling, next fall a perennial bed will be planted out front.

Maybe they exploit her, their little lamb, but they also love her, cherish her, and in their fevered, festering minds, whoever isn't engaged in avenging her death is in some sense a factor in having caused it.

FIVE

DIANE WAS THE ONE to greet her and Addie the next morning. Good. All the teachers at Lenox Nursery School were capable, trained, creative, loving, which is no more than you expect of the place where you put yourself on the waiting list the day the child is born, and where you now leave her for ten hours each day. But it was Diane who signaled Addie as her favorite. She never made the mistake of saying so. In that crucial ten minutes at the end of the day, when the parents arrived to pick up their children, and the children were weary or overexcited or, for reasons of their own, determinedly hostile, and the hum in the four bright rooms rose to a perceptibly higher level, in that disheveled interval Diane simply found occasion to relate the saga of Addie's achievements. Not just the standard report that all parents received—Good appetite at lunch, Pushed Peter off the swing, Needs another sweater for the playground—but the kind of commentary only a truly appreciative observer can amass. "In the sandbox she makes up these little songs." "She and her doll had a tea party in the woods." "She drew a butterfly with a crown on." ...And Diane's eyes glowing as she speaks, with that proprietary look that spells concern, that spells admiration, that spells love.

At first Lydia was conscience-stricken. It was unfair. Unfair for Diane. For her to squander all that affection on a child who in the natural course of events would be out of her life in another two years. She felt it as a species of theft. Lydia Ness stealing from this fervent young teacher whose feelings coincided with her own.

But of course that's absurd. There is no overall supply of affection that is diminished as its proprietor doles it out. There is, rather, an infinitely renewable supply, so that the love Diane focuses on Addie, far from detracting from any lifetime quota, enhances what she will be able to feel for the next enchanting three-year-old, and the next, and possibly, some man having discerned the endearing soul under that thick-waisted figure and the heavy features, some child of her own.

What a relief! To be able to accept the adulatory talk without a prod from vigilant conscience. Adulation that was doubly important inasmuch as there was no husband to share it with. Sometimes she thought that was the worst deprivation attached to single parenthood: you have no one to concur in the fatuous judgements. She's the prettiest . . . smartest . . . cutest . . . You can't say it to the other mothers as they stand collecting their children, or to the properly impartial teachers, or even to your good friend Pat who lives three floors above and whose five-year-old is sufficiently advanced as not to be touched by the comparison. Once she tried with Owen when he brought Addie back after one of the rare weekends. "She's really, um, pretty remarkable, isn't she?"

Owen agreed. "Remarkable. I'll say. Marcy and I took her to this restaurant, I thought it would be murder, but Marcy said let's give it a try, and do you know the child sat there without a move through the whole meal. Three courses. Not a peep out of her. Even the maître d', he said he'd never seen a child with such perfect manners." And Douglas was similarly obtuse when he'd spent an afternoon with them. "Good kid, don't you think?" she couldn't stop herself from prodding when Addie finally went off to bed. "Oh, great kid, great," Douglas said in his hearty way. "When you went off that time to get ice cream cones I tested her on the alphabet and damned if that child can't say the whole thing. A to Z. Letter perfect."

Useless. They both see the wrong thing. For Owen, it's the show of stilted manners that any three-year-old can put on under tension, and that a mother pays for later; and for Douglas, literal Douglas, the little show-off tricks that signify nothing except an aptitude for docile concentration. But as for discerning the imaginative wonders, the bright spurts of invention, only a working parent can do that. A working parent and, of course, someone like Diane, who is not ashamed to wear her infatuated heart on her professional sleeve.

When Lydia went to the door, Diane was straightening Addie's overalls. They were green overalls, faded, boyish, unadorned. It was not what Lydia first put on her this morning. She first put on a pink sunsuit embroidered with green and white flowers that tied in bows on Addie's shoulders. Then she looked at her child: the rosy skin, the brown hair cut straight in

bangs, the amazing brown eyes set off by that tender
pink, and all at once she was back in the parking lot,
she was hearing the note of menace in Maureen's hating voice: Suppose it was your daughter. "Mommy?"
Addie queried as the hasty hands undressed her.
"Mommy?" But by that time the sunsuit was on the
floor, the green overalls were buttoned up. Still cute,
but at least not a picture to tear your heart, compel
from the casual onlooker a stunned attention.

"Bye," she called now. No one turned. The school
had bought some toy shopping carts, yellow and purple and red, and Addie and her friend Sadie Lee were
each pushing one. "In our house we need chocolate-
chip ice cream and peanut butter and Band-Aids," she
could hear Addie say. She watched as the carts were
trundled across the room. In a few years Addie would
ask permission to go to the store alone. "But,
Mommy, all the kids my age are allowed to go shopping by themselves." And after that it would be dates.
"His name is Billy and he really is cute. Oh, well, I
don't really know his last name, but honestly, Mom,
he's very nice." How do mothers survive? She stood
at the door, but none of those preoccupied teachers
came over. They're not supposed to come over. This
is how partings from parents should be: easy, casual,
unattended by tears and messy sentiment. But as she
put her hand on the doorknob she thought that today, just today, she'd have welcomed a little sentiment. Enough so someone would walk over, pat her,
say, Don't worry, nothing bad will happen to her. Not
now and not when she's a beautiful eighteen-year-old
either. Just that gratuitous crumb, to give support.

Instead, she's the one slated to be supportive. Supportive, stern, sensible, full of practiced advice and timely admonition. Jerry was waiting at her office when she got there, his face solemn but also touched with that appealing half smile to which half a dozen people had paid tribute. The smile broadened when she told him about them.

"And they'll all testify? Even Chipper? Even Mrs. Forbes? She has a bad leg, it's really hard for her to get around."

"They'll all testify." She paused. She laid on the desk the list of messages her secretary had given her. "I also saw the family. Two of that family. Pam's sisters. I went to look at the parking lot and they drove by and guessed who I was."

"Not so nice for you, Miss Ness." A young man ready with the appropriate sympathy. "Did they give you a rough time?"

"Well, sure they gave me a rough time, why shouldn't they?" Her voice sounded strange in her own ears. "What else would you expect? They're devastated, those people. They live with the horror, it's with them always, they can't get it out of their minds."

"Well..." He looked puzzled. He's never heard her talk like this before. Well, she never has talked like this before.

"That's how it'll be at the trial, and you might as well be ready for it. They'll all be there, her whole enormous family. Oh, maybé not all of them at once, they have families of their own, jobs, commitments. But packs of them, all staring at you, hating you. The mother and father every day, and different sets of children with them. I know it, that's how it works. They all sit there in the front row, wearing their pain on their faces. Pain and hate. Pain and hate."

He stepped back. The smile that made Fern eager to jump into bed with him, that caused people to gravitate to him when he stood behind the counter, that kept Neils and Mrs. Forbes from letting him know how incompetent he could be... that smile was gone. "But I didn't do it."

"Oh, my God. Everyone who sits where you're sitting now says he didn't do it. Everyone. Some weep as they swear to it, some say it with great disdain, as if the very idea is unthinkable as connected with someone like them, some say it simply, with true drama. Innocent babes. But believe me, they all say it. Here and at the trial."

"I don't understand."

"I mean that whole family will be looking at you. The sick father and the mother who had a stroke, and the sisters and brothers and in-laws, and maybe some children of their own if they're grown up enough, and I don't know who all, and they won't give a damn what you say. They'll be thinking as family, not as logical people. They won't even listen to the testimony about what a nice, upright young man you are. They'll want to tear you limb from limb. Revenge. That's what they'll want, and you're the one to get it from."

"But the jury, isn't that who—"

"The jury are parents too. People with children, grandchildren, nieces, nephews. You can't keep off the

jury everyone who's ever worried when a beloved
daughter was late getting home, it isn't possible. Those
human beings on the jury, they'll be attending to the
witnesses, sure they will, but they'll also be looking at
those faces in the front row, identifying with them.
Same thing when you're testifying—the jury will be
looking at them, that wounded family. Not at you.
You'll panic. You'll forget what the two of us worked
over. You won't know what you're saying anymore.''

"Miss Ness, what are you saying? That I'll be convicted! Me, Jerry Eldstrom! I'll go to prison for life!''

Yes, what is she saying? To turn this nice young
man into a zombie, so his skin has gone gray and his
eyes bulge with fright and the motion of the table on
which his hand is resting shows how he is trembling.
What got into her, so for a minute she stopped being
a defense attorney, she was the mother of a child in a
pink sunsuit? She is the one, identifying with those
front-row faces. Suppose it was your daughter. Well,
she did suppose it, and for a moment it sent her over
the edge; she behaved as it's impermissible for a lawyer to behave.

She walked over to the window. "Jerry, I just
wanted to sketch in the worst-possible-case scenario.'' Her voice was back to normal. Assertive,
steady. She said they had a list of witnesses the prosecution was going to call, she wanted to go over it with
him. There weren't many. A neighbor who would
doubtless testify to the restricted nature of Pam's life.
Another who would say the same thing, thus establishing the unlikelihood of the girl's going out with a
man she didn't know. Pam's father. The two sisters

who had been in the house on the fatal night. A neighbor of Mrs. Forbes, a Mrs. Lateen. The clerk at Neils' who had heard Jerry make the ill-advised offer to drive the girl home.

"That drive, that may well be the most damaging thing against you. The prosecutor will hammer away at it. Mr. Eldstrom, is it your habit to offer to drive customers home with their purchases? Did you ever drive a customer home before? Does Mr. Neils encourage his salesmen to drive customers home? Did Miss Howells ask you to drive her home, or was the offer entirely your own idea? Isn't it a fact, Mr. Eldstrom"—her voice rising, thickened—"that you made the offer because you expected she would be alone in the house, and you were surprised by the unexpected arrival of her father?"

Like the performer she could be, she shot the questions at him. That was how the prosecutor would put it, she said. Cutting, insinuating. That was what he had to get ready for.

"But it's not true, none of it." His voice was quiet; he also was making an effort to cross out that earlier episode. "I only said I'd drive her home because she looked so pitiful standing there, trying to lift those heavy cans. I was sorry for her, I told you."

"You'll have to tell the court."

"Besides, why would I want to be alone with her in a house? I didn't even like being alone with her in the car," he said earnestly. "She was such a—well, she wore this flowered dress. No shape. Like a jumper, but not exactly a jumper. And her hair, hanging straight down. Anyhow, not just her looks. That way she had of talking. When I first met her—I explained this—I thought she was fifteen. But not one of those cute fifteen-year-olds. Someone who's, I don't know how to say it, not quite all there. No spark. No spirit. She was a zero. A drip. Can I speak frankly?'' he said: the nice young man again. ''She turned me off. I wouldn't want to be in bed with her, no man in his right mind would, I don't care how hard up he is.''

She told her secretary no, she wouldn't answer that call. ''Jerry, you can speak frankly here, but you'd better not speak the same way in court. This is a dead woman we're talking about. A woman who's been sanctified by her family. Whatever she was in real life, she's a saint by now—you can't insult a saint. It's a thin line, I admit, we have to walk, but we damn well better stick to it. Our defense has to be predicated on the fact that you're not the kind to assault a girl. We steer away from the fact that she's not the kind of girl a red-blooded man would want to assault. So let's go over the question again. Isn't it a fact, Mr. Eldstrom, that you thought she was going to be alone in the house, and that's why you made that wholly unaccustomed offer to drive her home?''

They went over a lot of questions. She read from a list the kind of query the prosecutor would put, and he, being helpful and also more nervous than before, worked at the answers. Then she looked at her notes. ''Jerry, we're still going to have our biggest headache, I think, with that drive. So I just wondered. Suppose we could say that you were due someplace at six-thirty that evening. Someplace pressing. A person, maybe, you wouldn't want to let down. Or even a party. That would go a long way to showing that you had no intention of, um, spending time with the girl.''

It had started to rain, a warm June downpour, and he kept his eyes on the drops streaming down her window. There was nothing like that, he said.

''Where did you go when you left Pam's house?''

He pulled at his ear. He went to have dinner with his parents, he said. He was right on the way. Oak Lane is two blocks from the highway to Pendil Park.

''Ah.'' She tried to keep the disappointment out of her voice. A mother testifying that her son was rushing so he would be on time for dinner with her; no use at all.

Then she thought of something. ''Didn't you tell me you went to see your parents on Sundays? And the day you drove Pam''—she checked her notes—''March twelfth. A Thursday.''

''This time I was going home on Thursday,'' he said in the pleasant voice that could have a touch of stubbornness.

''Jerry, think back. Can't you do better than that? Was it one of their birthdays? Their anniversary? Or just a casual whim?''

''It wasn't casual, I had to get him home.''

''Him?''

He blushed. He fiddled with the ashtray on her desk. He straightened a pile of her papers. ''Silly, calling a turkey 'he.' For all I know it was a she. There's this frozen-food locker near where I work, and my mother read that they were having a great special on frozen turkeys. Turkey in March, don't ask me. But that's my mother, she has about twenty recipes for leftover turkey. Anyhow, she asked me to bring her one.''

She sighed. Life—true life—is like that. Messy. Unobliging. Refusing to fall into the neat patterns that would make a defense lawyer's job easy. It's perfectly plausible, if not dramatically effective, that a young man who ordinarily went home for Sunday lunch this time did it for Thursday dinner so Mama could pick up a bargain on frozen turkey.

''Would anyone at the frozen-food place remember that you came in?''

He shook his head. All very impersonal, he said. The way most things are today. Which is why he tries so hard to put the personal element into transactions with customers at the hardware store.

''Something else,'' she said. ''That car. Fern told me that on the night of the murder the two of you didn't do the accustomed thing, which was go to a restaurant for dinner''—where someone could have seen you and changed the whole complexion of this trial, she forbore to add—''because your car was being fixed.''

''Right. What I told her.''

Lydia held her pencil above the pad. ''What garage did you take it to?'' And when he hesitated, she gave the usual reminder: a question the prosecutor would ask.

More waiting. The eager eyes looked downward. His fingers went out again to the ashtray. ''I didn't exactly tell the truth.'' Another pause. She could see his foot, in its brown loafer, do a tattoo against the leg of the chair. ''I didn't think it would matter. Thing is,

I was a little short of cash. Because of this date with another girl the night before. We went to this club, it totted up to more than I expected. But I didn't want to say that to Fern, naturally I didn't. And that little Spanish place we both like, it can take a bite out of a fifty-dollar bill. You order wine and a couple of drinks, and bingo. Good food, but they soak you.''

Like all nice people caught in deception, he was talking too much. She jabbed her pencil on the lined pad. ''So you gave the wrong information to the police?''

''Does it matter?''

''Christ, Jerry. You made a statement that's a lie— it's a prosecutor's dream come true. Shows you can lie about other things too. Why do you think they ask you questions at the police station? So they can give you a sandwich and send you nicely home? Think again. When they tell you anything you say will be used against you, they're not kidding. You convict yourself. You.''

Then she saw his face and calmed down. It's what you always have to do with defendants: tell them over and over everything matters. And you have to do it with patient tact, remembering that what is natural to you is alien to them; they've never been exposed to a trial before, they have no idea what it is to deal with a clever and determined prosecutor whose only aim is to trap them.

''Jerry, let's go back. You told the police you were having your car fixed, when all the time it was in good shape?''

"I'm sorry."

"And next morning, did you drive it to work?"

Next morning, he admitted, he did indeed drive it to work. "But it was just so that Fern...I mean, does she have to find out now that I— Don't answer that, Miss Ness. I know. I know."

She sighed. And where was his car on that fatal night?

Where it always was, he said. Parked on the block between Elm and Forrest, though sometimes if it's crowded there he has to cross over to Mayhew. No, he doesn't know that anyone would have seen it, when you park a car on one of those blocks where some people have their own garages and some don't, your aim is to stay inconspicuous. They make enough fuss as it is about overnight parking on the street—last thing you want is for someone to see you night after night and get an idea you're taking up too much room.

She made another note. He'd lied to the police about the car, which will provide an opening for the prosecutor to tear through, and he lied to Fern, which signifies nothing. Thousands of young men find it desirable to conceal from a girl their relationship with some other girl—sometimes, who knows, the girl wants to be deceived, conspires in her own deception. It doesn't make him a rapist. All it does is make his attorney's job harder. She closed the notebook, where the entries were becoming more full. When she'd stopped in to see Ben this morning and give him a rundown, he said from the sound of it her client did indeed seem cloaked in innocence. The cloak is still an actuality, but sitting here she thinks that some of its seams may be crooked, and if anyone looks closely, they just might consider that it is frayed around the edges.

SIX

NO MATTER HOW OFTEN she goes through it, the first day of a trial is always a panic, a heart stopper. Always the same apprehensive flutters, the same disorderly push of thought: Can I carry it off? Will the jury like me? Would it help if I changed my hairstyle? If I flub it, a man will go to jail for life. But she was used to trials in New York City, where part of the rite is the walk through the lobby of 100 Centre Street, the confrontation with an assemblage that consists of defense lawyers, policemen, prosecuting attorneys, defendants, defendants' families, and most of all the indeterminate groups whose resigned faces and indolent poses manifest their willingness to hang out there, if necessary, round the clock.

Here, when she stepped out of the car, she was conscious of a great expanse of blue sky, of the hint of an ocean breeze, of a gaudy row of gladiolus bordering the walk to the courthouse steps, and, when she went inside, though photographers and TV men were scattered around the hall, people looked quiet and composed. The issues might be the same—life and death—but the trappings were low-key. Even when she and the prosecuting attorney—a middle-aged man called Martin Clay—met in the judge's chambers, there seemed to her a substratum of good will. The judge called them in to discuss the ground rules—how many

seats reserved for the press, how many alternates for
the jury, would both sides waive their rights to ask for
a change of venue—but as they stood flanked by his
green leather armchairs, cooled by the air from his air
conditioners, she felt along with the competitiveness
an emanation of cordiality, as if everything were con-
spiring to make the city attorney feel at ease. It even
turned out that the man who had courteously waited
to hold the door open for her as she came up the steps
was Clay's assistant.

"So far so good," she said to Tony when they were
seated at the counsel's table. But then the breath
caught in her throat. Cordiality! What's wrong with
her! She looked over at the front row and discovered
for herself what she had tried to explain to Jerry: no
way to ignore the claims of those sitting there. A
funereal row—well, to them it was a type of funeral—consisting of a stooped woman who had to be
Pam's mother, and a gaunt man who was surely the
father, and two women who must be sisters because
they had the family insignia—the saucer-shaped eyes,
the flat, glossy forehead, the dimply mouth that could
be both prim and flirtatious at once—and a younger
man who, Lydia realized, despite his creased face and
puffy eyes was a brother. They did a lot of bustling
around—a sister arranged a black shawl around the
mother's shoulders, and the other, an excessively stout
one, got up to fetch a paper cup of water for the father, and then the first sister searched in her pocketbook for a tissue for the mother, and the brother
passed down a roll of peppermints for both parents,

and in each of these motions there was an affirmation of agony, a tacit rebuke.

Lydia sat holding a pencil over her yellow lined pad. Once, to terminate one of those mother-daughter rows that are a feature of the early adolescent years, her mother slipped on the kitchen floor and pulled a tendon in her ankle, and now the pit of Lydia's stomach suddenly remembered the sour looks: martyrdom writ large in the heavy eyes and stifled groans as her mother stumbled painfully around the house doing the chores that didn't need to be done. Her fault, her fault. When she looked again, the shawl was off the mother—the air-conditioning, at least in these early stages, was less efficacious here than in the judge's chambers—and a new man had been added to the row: one whose square face and wide, toothy mouth barred him from being a blood relation. A friend? A husband? The husband of the stout sister, Lydia inferred, from the looks at once chastising and relieved that accompanied his arrival. Indeed, they all settled in relief when he came, which didn't stop him, once the voir dire began, from unfolding his newspaper and reading.

The judge opened the voir dire with some standard remarks. Standard but, to her mind, comforting: "We realize how much publicity has attached to this case," he told the panel. "Obviously, counsel don't expect to find men and women who've never heard about the crime. You've all been reading the papers, you've talked to your neighbors, you've undoubtedly formed opinions. What counsel on both sides are looking for is people who can lay such opinions aside and make judgments based strictly on the evidence we're going to hear. Also, people who in making these judgments won't concede too quickly on their own views or resist too strongly someone else's persuasion.''

Sometimes she talks to a friend who for one reason or another has attended a trial, and invariably they make the same comment about the voir dire: boring, boring. She can see their point. The big decisions, after all, are not made in front of the spectators or explained to them. They don't know why a potential juror has been challenged, or for what reasons, or which side has done the challenging, or whether a juror has been excused with a peremptory challenge or a challenge for cause. They simply observe a great tide of people that shrinks, increases, shrinks, without apparent rationale. Up there on the screen, the action goes on but the titles are missing.

On the other hand, for her it is a time of nervous exhilaration. Her last chance to have a dialogue with men and women who will decide her case. She talks, they talk back. Tell me about the time you were mugged, Mrs. Smith: interaction. A chance for rapport. Once the trial begins, all that ends. She talks, the prosecutor talks, the witnesses talk, the jury sits silent and judgmental.

She has never felt the need of a social psychologist to help her in jury selection. Sufficient, it seems to her, are the common-sense edicts—in a case of arson, you don't choose someone whose house burned down last week—plus her own intuitive hunches, plus canny utilization of any surprises that may emerge. There were few surprises in this crowd. Everyone had felt the nasty pinch of crime: the usher in a movie theater who twice had her purse stolen as she walked home after midnight, the electrician sent to fix wiring in a building where a drug bust was in progress, the man who gave up his small candy store because the kids coming in after school would rob him blind. And all declared roundly that these experiences would not interfere with their ability to have an open mind. Their protests sounded credible. They had to sound credible, or where would you be?

At twelve the judge declared a recess, and Jerry turned to her. "I'm sorry, Miss Ness."

"Sorry?"

"All these unpleasant stories, you won't get such a good idea of our town."

She looked at him in amazement. He's apologizing for North Rainey. A defendant in a murder trial, and he's expressing regret for the casual shabbiness to which his home town has exposed her. He wants to keep things pleasant for her: Jerry, still the perpetual salesman.

She said in New York City, where she usually practiced, the experience of crime would be worse.

"Yeah. I guess so. Things aren't so hot in Pendil Park either, where my parents live. Miss Ness, I want you to meet my father."

Well, of course she wants to meet his father; she wished there had been time before this. She'd glanced at the spectators in the two front rows and wondered which were Jerry's parents.

But the man who approached came laboriously from a seat in the middle of the courtroom. He really thanked her, he said. He and Mrs. Eldstrom both. Her taking the case—it made them both breathe easier.

He looked like Jerry: the same even features and courteous gaze and diffident half smile—now that she saw him, of course she would pick him out. But he was shorter than Jerry, slighter, with a little twitch that from time to time tugged at one bright blue eye.

Lydia said carefully that she thought they had a good case.

"Oh, I'm sure, Miss Ness. I'm very sure." He didn't look sure. He looked timorous, troubled, awed by the trappings of officialdom he saw all around. His abject gaze followed the spectators as they walked out, as if they too might be empowered to decide Jerry's fate. Then he turned toward the door through which the judge was departing. "Do you think that judge likes Jerry?"

"I think he'll give him a fair trial."

"How about those jurors? They're not especially friendly, are they?"

"If they were, Mr. Eldstrom, the prosecutor would have ample cause to disqualify them."

"I don't know. That electrician. He looked sort of mean."

Actually, she'd been hoping she could keep the electrician; as one exposed in the course of his work to a wide variety of customers to whom it was politic to be civil, he might well sympathize with Jerry's misguided civility to Pam—it was Clay who would probably challenge him. She didn't say this. It was as well not to go into the minutiae of jury selection with your clients, and surely not with their relatives. Instead, she said she hoped in future Mr. Eldstrom would sit in the front row.

"I didn't want to be conspicuous." He eased up against a bench as he spoke, as though still trying to efface himself.

"Oh, listen. Jerry's parents ought to be conspicuous. The jury should get to see you the way they see that other family. They should be conscious every minute of how much you care about your son."

"How much we care! You mean they think we don't?" His voice shook; the two old men who are a staple of every courtroom turned around to look at him. "But we were the ones, Vera and I, who told Jerry he had to change lawyers, that other fellow wasn't doing enough."

She nodded; it was the kind of comment Jerry might make. Eager, sincere, and also slightly obtuse. "I know that, Mr. Eldstrom. Mr. Lyttle knows it. But the jury won't. The way they won't automatically know the sacrifices you made to get us. We can't tell them about your great concern, but we can show them. We can have on display for them day after day the caring, loving people Jerry has for parents."

The twitch, for an instant, disfigured the clear blue gaze. She reminded herself that he was a pharmacist—doubtless a good one. Behind his own counter, translating the indecipherable jottings, typing the categorical labels, he would be a man with authority. Now even the word *parents* seemed to throw him. "My wife—she couldn't come today."

"That's all right. I guess she'll come tomorrow."

He nodded; this time his hands twitched. Did Miss Ness like ginger? he asked.

"Ginger?"

"Vera's making some for you. Ginger candy. It's her specialty."

Ginger candy when a son is on trial for rape and murder. Lydia said she did like ginger candy—at the same time, the thought crossed her mind of Jerry working all Sunday morning to fix Mrs. Forbes's pipes, which then leaked worse than ever on Monday. Well-meaning ineptitude—does it really run in families? "Mr. Eldstrom, it was a pleasure to meet you. And don't forget. The front row this afternoon."

She walked alone through the hall. Such a quiet hall, so different from the halls in the Criminal Courts building in New York, where every turn in a corridor gives you a new drama, another scene of heartbreak or outrage or stunned resignation. Such solidity here, she thought. Such a sense of justice presiding. But then she passed a door that said PART 3, and though the door was closed, she could hear the shouting inside. "Yeah, I could so see him even though the lights were out," an irate voice said clearly. All right, not so solid after all—Douglas would have plenty to say in disapproval.

Douglas had asked once or twice if he could listen to her at a trial. She'd seen the buildings he worked on, he said; why shouldn't he be able to observe her work? He knew she must be great; it would give him real pleasure. She said, "Sorry, Doug, but no." "I understand," he'd said. "You want to be free to be corny or sarcastic or melodramatic without being afraid I might be critical of all that showy acting.'' Douglas was wrong. It was not in the least that she feared his judgment. What she feared was her consciousness of an alien presence impinging for even a second on her concentration.

No one realized how you had to concentrate. One of her college roommates, a beautiful girl named Grace, was now a psychoanalyst, and she liked to compare their respective careers. ''It's different with you, Lyddy,'' she'd say. ''You know exactly where everything is going. You have the questions laid out in advance, you brief the witnesses, you don't even ask a question—isn't that the accepted rule?—unless you're sure of the answer. It's exactly the opposite with us. Free association. We have no idea where the patient is heading or what's going to turn out to be crucial. That's why attentiveness is all. We sit there looking passive, but we're really concentrating like crazy. In all that irreverent stream, what word will they let slip, what tiny clue, to put the whole thing in perspective?'' Lydia didn't argue, not with Grace, but she thought, What does she know? We concentrate just as much. We can have the whole scenario written out, each answer labeled and weighed and predicted, and still it can be that inadvertent word, that little misstep, that makes the difference.

When she went back to court, she had to face the fact that Pam's family was disturbing her concentration. All that posturing and grimacing and fidgeting that was the outer manifestation of their pain. Did they do it purposely, to distract her? Of course not. What an idea. But she was distracted. When the

mother coughed and the two sisters on either side
leaned over to pat her, when the father rubbed his
head as if in torment and the brother took his hand,
when that square-faced son-in-law at the end brought
in two more cups of water, when they moved their
knees to make room for a newcomer to sit next to
Mama, she knew what they were saying. She knew.

The newcomer was Amy. Lydia had been waiting
for a new juror to walk up, and for a second she
turned, and her gaze met that level one. Maybe Amy
would nod. Not a greeting, but an infinitesimal ac-
knowledgment. Hadn't they worked out their hostility, after all, on that barren parking field? No, they
had not worked out their hostility; settling herself,
kissing her parents, hugging a sister, Amy wore the
same accusing look as the rest of them, the same air of
bitter judgment.

The new juror was a carpenter who said it would be
hard for him to give a few weeks because he was paid
for when he worked and only for that. And after him
a housewife who said both her daughters had been
married at eighteen. She objected then, but the way
things were nowadays, all these terrible crimes, she
figured that was not at all a bad idea; settle them down
and you knew they were safe. And after her a young
woman who ran a children's bookstore. A young intelligent woman who lived alone, sometimes stayed
alone in the store after her assistant left, kept the door
locked because that was prudent but couldn't remember a time when she had refused entrance to anyone,
even a single, young, disheveled-looking male. Did she
ever have trouble? Well, people stole books if she

didn't watch them, you'd be surprised, the most motherly respectable types were not above slipping a volume or two into their pocketbooks, but no, no trouble like that, not ever.

She was too good to be true: Clay would surely challenge her, Lydia thought. In her annoyance at this, she pressed doubly hard at the next juror, who was a truck driver and looked it: hard, ruddy, an incipient belly above the belt. Did he understand what was meant by the term "presumption of innocence"? Did he know the burden was on the prosecution to prove guilt beyond a reasonable doubt? The man nodded, Yes, yes, he knew, but resonating louder than his dutiful mumble was a groan from the front row. She didn't turn, but her mind's eye presented her with a picture of the man who'd made it. The gaunt cheeks, the stricken eyes, the furrows pulled across the wide forehead—the forehead that Pam had so assiduously stroked. Innocence! that groan was saying. Don't talk to this father about innocence.

"So how do you think it went?" Tony asked when they finally got in the car to go home.

"I don't know. Doesn't seem like such a bad pool. He'll have a jury of his peers, that's for sure." She was tired; she closed her eyes. Then that furrowed forehead intruded, and she opened them. "Tony, are you on speaking terms with the Greek myths?"

"Myths?" He turned his boyish-looking face.

"Vengeance," she said. "That's the main thing. Someone is always seeking vengeance because of something terrible that was done to them. Being avenged: what life is for. Minos decreed that seven youths and seven maidens from Athens had to be given him every year to throw to the monster because his son was killed in Athens, and Creon said Polynices's body had to lie unburied to be devoured by the birds and beasts because of something I forget, and Medea, well, you surely know about her vengeance.''

Tony shook his head. ''I played chess all through high school. Five, six hours a day. Even in class. If any teacher ever talked about Medea, I was playing a chess game in my head.''

''Well, Medea,'' she said. ''Medea charmed the serpent who guarded her father's Golden Fleece so Jason could steal it. Then she killed her own brother and threw his limbs into the sea so she could flee with Jason, who promised to marry her and love her forever. She did other awful deeds for Jason's sake too, and she bore him two children. Sons. But then Jason showed the meanness that was in him. He got engaged to marry the daughter of the king of Corinth.'' The car rounded a corner, and Lydia saw from the alert tilt of his head that Willis was also listening from up front. She raised her voice.

''So there was Medea, far from her home, brooding about her wretchedness and wanting to be revenged. But she was a resolute and able woman; she didn't just sit back and wait. She took from her chest a beautiful robe and anointed it with deadly drugs and had her young sons take it to the princess as a gift. But no sooner did the princess put it on than she was devoured by a fearful fire and dropped dead; all her flesh had melted away.'' The tilt of Willis's head grew more pronounced; as they eased into the line for the tunnel, he even drove more slowly—what was coming next? Lydia suddenly realized what was coming next. Why did she ever start this! Medea, for God's sake! Didn't she know what she would be getting into? Was this really the time to allude to those two young sons? She put her head back on the leather seat. "That's it," she said flatly. "That's the story of how one woman got her vengeance."

SEVEN

TWO DAYS LATER, the jury was chosen. *Cordiality* was no longer the word she'd have used to describe the relations between her and Clay—he plainly was affronted, and several times said so, by her attempts to establish a rapport with potential jurors—but at least there was no outright contention. She had tried for jurors on the young side, on the assumption that they would not impute a bad character to a young man whose defense in part was going to be that he enjoyed sex with a willing girl friend; and she also hoped for a certain degree of sophistication, or at least intelligence. The final line-up was promising. Among them was an accountant for a music company, a postman, a physical education teacher (male), a telephone repair person (female), a housewife, a chef at a fast-food restaurant, a nurse's aide, a nurse, a rug salesman. Two were black—two out of twelve, which, she reflected, was almost the opposite proportion she'd have had in New York. One of the blacks was the housewife, a woman in her sixties whom Lydia accepted because her three daughters all worked as school-teachers, which bespoke a degree of family sophistication. The other was the telephone repair person, a young woman who went unescorted to a wide variety of dwellings and had never, as she grandly put it, seen any reason to be scared. Lydia thought

Clay would use a challenge on her as he did on the bookstore owner, but he let her pass, and there she sat, the twelfth juror, with her Afro hairstyle and her valiant spirit. And surely it was true that Jerry had a jury of his peers; if he was more educated than the mailman, he was less so than the accountant and the phys. ed. teacher.

The courtroom was more crowded for the opening statements, and the left side of the front row was also full: a redheaded sister she hadn't seen before and a pale man with indeterminate features who might be a brother but also might be someone's husband. But otherwise the same line-up: drooping mother, gaunt father, grieving siblings. Counting the new sister, she had now seen nine of them. Nine siblings and spouses out of a possible eighteen. And in the front row across the aisle, with an empty seat on either side, Jerry's father.

Jerry's mother had come yesterday. Lydia had hoped for a tableau for the benefit of the jury, both parents on hand to hug their son after the jurors were sworn in, but only the mother was present. It somehow depressed her, and the encounter with Mrs. Eldstrom in the hall depressed her further. Where Mr. Eldstrom had been diffident and obtuse, Mrs. Eldstrom was effusive and brash. She was a stout woman with a pile of curly hair and a flowered silk dress plainly chosen for its festive qualities. Only a pasty tint to her complexion and circles under her eyes spoke of private anguish.

And she made her feelings clear right away. "He's innocent, you know. No way my son Jerry could do that kind of thing."

She was certainly going to try to convince the jury of that, Lydia said.

"It's obvious. All they have to do is look at him." The woman spoke truculently, as if offering a suggestion not yet thought of.

"I'm afraid that won't be quite enough," Lydia murmured.

"Won't you tell them how good he is? Always has been. That boy, I don't think he ever did a mean thing in his life."

"Mrs. Eldstrom, we have a list of character witnesses. People he works with, friends, his landlady, I'm sure Jerry told you." Two passing reporters slowed down, plainly eager to listen in on this timely conversation, and she steered Mrs. Eldstrom over toward a window.

"If you'd call me, I'd tell them a thing or two."

"I'd love to call you. Unfortunately, a mother talking about how virtuous and wonderful her son is doesn't cut much ice with a jury."

"But it's so unreasonable. There's not even a case. No one can prove a thing." When she reached into her pocketbook, Lydia thought it might be for that promised ginger candy, but that was evidently Mr. Eldstrom's fiction because only a handkerchief came out.

Lydia sighed. "Let me tell you what happens. After the prosecutor presents his case, we'll ask the judge for a verdict of acquittal. You know, for him to dismiss the charges on the ground that there isn't enough evidence. So if there's—''

''He'll do it, won't he? If he has any sense, won't he do it?''

''I surely hope he will. But I have to admit it's very rare for that to happen. We can't let ourselves count on it.''

''We put a second mortgage on our house just to get you. We'll do anything. If it's more money...'' Her hand trembled as she put back the handkerchief, and, Lydia thought, this woman isn't as brash as she sounds. She's terrified. Her big talk is all bravado.

She put her arm around the shoulder encased in silk. ''Look. The best thing you can do, you and Mr. Eldstrom, is come regularly. Show by your presence how much Jerry means to you. The jury will get the point. They'll read your expression. They'll identify with your worry. They'll know this is a young man whose parents think the world of him.''

But they hadn't come. Yesterday it was Mrs. Eldstrom, and today, for the opening statements, Mr. Eldstrom again. Mr. Eldstrom and, as she couldn't forget, the others, while Clay in his stagy but also chummy words went through the saga of what he intended to prove.

There were few surprises. A girl, after all, had been raped and killed; Clay simply touched on the facts that had been set down and embellished and repeated in the papers. The deserted parking lot. The green car. The license number on the green car. The medical examiner's finding of sexual assault. But what he came down on hardest was the personality of the girl. The strained and, to an unprejudiced mind, Lydia thought, distorted personality. She never went out. Pam liked staying home. If she did baby-sitting, it was for her sisters' or brothers' children. She enjoyed the small domestic chores. She resisted all overtures of friendliness. And— "As I will have witnesses to prove, ladies and gentlemen" —she would never have got into a car with anyone she didn't know well: that was the clincher. And the man she knew well— "I will present testimony to confirm this, ladies and gentlemen"—was Jerry. She didn't just know him, she trusted him. Somehow he had touched that susceptible core that lay deep within the timorous exterior. She was willing to drive home with him when her cans of paint were heavy. She would let him carry them to the front door and then into the house. It was debatable who had suggested the visit to her room—since there was only the word of the defendant, that was something the jury would have to decide—but in any case, her father's arrival home rendered that visit an uneventful one. And it was a fact that when she heard his name on the phone, she was willing to go out with him. Hopefully, in deference to her sisters' suggestions, she changed her clothes: she put on a different scarf; she went upstairs for a different pair of shoes. Then, with an expectant look on her face, this innocent girl, ladies and gentlemen, opened the door, she went down the front steps, she—

Clay didn't relate what happened next because Mrs. Howells fainted. At least the head that had been leaning against Amy's shoulder fell precipitously forward. Someone behind her shrieked. People from rows behind craned their necks. The court artist scribbled furiously. The court clerk ran back. The judge asked if they wanted assistance.

Two minutes later, the woman was upright again. The recovery involved more bustling. Maureen went for water, the brother leaned over to wipe the pallid brow, the new sister, whose name turned out to be Donna—"Donna, don't you have smelling salts?"—took this item out of her pocketbook and held it under her mother's nose. Clay had been quiet during all this, but he finished fast. He might well finish fast, Lydia thought. They had provided the tag line for him, one calculated to wring every drop of drama and pathos out of an already shocking story.

And what did they have in store for her? If they would provide a faint for an ally, what would they do for the enemy? She started with careful deliberation—"I'm going to make it clear, ladies and gentlemen, that my client had nothing to do with that terrible crime"—but part of her mind was on them. When would it start? What was their tactic?

Their tactic was boredom. While she talked—Mr. Eldstrom had been at Fern Eaton's that evening, Mr. Eldstrom had an indisputable reputation for honor, Mr. Eldstrom was respected by his colleagues—they sat languid. No fainting, not even the usual bustling. They were simply a study in venomous fatigue, as if what she was saying was at once tedious and trivial. Donna of the smelling salts held her hand to her forehead. Amy yawned. Stacy leaned her head on the shoulder of her husband's blue and white striped seersucker suit and closed her eyes. Had Clay advised them? No, she thought, they operated independently of Clay. It simply came to them that this was the best way to belittle the defense attorney's words. A tactic embodying distaste and surprise. "...know when you've heard it all, you'll decide he's an estimable young man who would never have committed so barbaric an act." When she finished and sat down, Jerry leaned toward her. "Thanks for all those nice things," he said with his open smile. Amazing; he was oblivious. He didn't see them. Not their posturing, not their grimacing, not the expressions that were the confirmation of their convulsive anger. Like an invalid, he had developed a protective egocentricity. He knew only what directly pertained to himself. His trail, his destiny, the nice things said about himself.

He did wince, however, as Clay launched into his case, introducing first the policeman who had found the body and then the medical examiner, who relayed in detail what its injuries were. Lydia did raise protests here. The gruesome details—of course they were part of the record. The bloodstained brick—obviously a legitimate exhibit. Even photographs of the site itself, its dismal stretches and secluded corners and the warning sign on its gate—granted. But pictures of the poor, desecrated body—Lydia objected that this was needlessly inflammatory without adding to basic information, and the judge sustained her.

Then the promised parade of witnesses started, to prove first that Pam would not have got into a car with a man she didn't know, and second that the only man she knew was Jerry. Over a two-day period, there were plenty of eager friends and neighbors. "We always saw her walking alone." "Lots of times she'd be sitting on the porch by herself." "I once invited her for a cup of tea but she said no." Under Clay's prodding, it even turned out that one neighbor (53 Oak Lane) had brought a young man over. "She was so sweet and pretty, I thought it was a shame, a young girl like that never going out. So I asked Mrs. Howells, and she said okay with her. So I came over one night with this young nephew. My husband's sister's boy, but he was staying with us that month because... Oh, I see. I guess you don't need that. Anyhow, such a nice fellow. Bobby. Shy, like she was. Quiet. Nice manners. Nothing to frighten her. And Pam came down from her room and I introduced them, and her mother put out some cookies. She had on this blue dress and that soft blond hair—I could see Bobby liked her. But then she went back upstairs. No reason. No one was even threatening to leave her and Bobby alone. But that's Pam for you. She just said, Excuse me, please, I have something to do, and off she went. So there we were, her mother and Bobby and me. What did she have to do, I wonder."

Lydia wondered, too. Or, rather, she wondered at the resolve that would keep a girl in paths of such impenetrable austerity. What had she seen of life to turn her against it? Was it something that had happened in her own home? Or in the home of one of those families who now sat embattled in their ordained row? Or was it simply innate, so while nine children in a family would feel comfortable dealing with the world, one would decide on a life of sacred withdrawal from it?

In any case, she raised few objections here, and even fewer when Clay started on the litany of Pam's relationship with Jerry. One salesman at Neils' after another, stumbling through the familiar recital: the girl came in and went to Jerry, who made suggestions to her, instructed her, cautioned her, explained to her the assets and dangers of particular products. It was fertile ground, and Clay dug into it. Was it really necessary to tell the girl she should wear gloves and open the windows when she used the chemical stripper? Were there instructions on the box advising people to take just such precautions? Did they themselves feel it incumbent on them to go into such details when they sold this product? Had they noticed whether Jerry exercised such solicitude with other customers?

She knew what Clay was trying to do: build up Jerry Eldstrom as seducer, as snake, as man worming his way into a young girl's trust. But she was not inclined to interrupt because she suspected that unawares he was also doing something else: sketching the portrait of every customer's dream salesman. At one time or other, everyone is in need of a mentor like Jerry. If it isn't to strip wallpaper from a wall, it's to cut a slipcover pattern or follow the blueprints for making a birdhouse. And at such daunting times, everyone feels overwhelmed by the same questions. How much do I need, which tool should I buy, what does this small print mean, who'll help me if I get stuck? And here, it turned out, was someone ready and willing to answer these questions, especially the last one. There he was, the personification of know-how and sufferance: not just the perpetual salesman but the perfect one. Which of those jurors had not on some occasion been wishing to find him?

Clay moved from Jerry's supposedly seductive ways to that damning car ride home—a session in which she and Clay repeatedly clashed, as he made insinuations that she as vehemently opposed—and finally to the night of the crime itself. It had been a long day. It was after three o'clock. She thought for so crucial a subject, the judge might call a recess until morning. But conscientious as ever, he waved Clay on, and Amy was called to give her story of Pam's first and last date.

"She was so excited, poor darling. When she hung up the phone, I mean. We asked her who Jerry was, and she couldn't tell us enough. So sweet and kind and sensitive, someone who really understood what she was trying to accomplish in her room and had given her all this help. And now he wanted her to go for a ride with him. A ride on this lovely night. It never occurred to her to ask questions. She didn't even think to change her clothes, that's what an innocent she was. She reached into the closet for something to put on her head, and she pulled out this old blue scarf she used to wear on chilly days for gardening—all torn and faded. She didn't even see what it looked like. So Stacy found another scarf, this plaid one some of the nieces gave her for Christmas, and she said okay, she'd wear that. And then her shoes. She had on some sort of ballet slippers. Paper-thin soles, when it was almost freezing outside. So we told her to go up and change. And I wanted to say, 'Why doesn't he come in and meet the family?' but you know, with her looking all starry-eyed, well, I just couldn't. I remembered one

time she was in high school and she said she was going
for a walk with a boy. Hallelujah. Pam with a boy.
And I asked the simplest question. I said, 'This boy,
did you meet him in one of your classes?' I didn't
mean anything by it. I wasn't checking up, Christ no.
Or doubting her judgment. Just making conversation. But it set her thinking. She stood still a minute,
and then she shook her head. 'I changed my mind,'
she said. 'Tell him I'm sick. Tell him I can't go.' And
I didn't want the same thing to happen again. After
all, a girl nineteen years old going out for the first
time, I didn't want to queer it. The light going out of
her eyes—I couldn't bear that. So I just said. 'Have
fun, honey,' I even opened the door for her. I opened
the door so my sister could go off and be killed.''

Amy didn't say all this at once. There was some judicious prodding from Clay, a few pauses for quiet
sobbing. But she got it out, and afterward Stacy went
over the same ground.

Stacy was the stout one, married to the square-faced
man. Lydia knew a lot about them by this time. From
studying the early clippings, listening, watching, she
had them pinned down. She could assign wives to
husbands, names to faces, in some cases, to occupa-
tions and locales. The Howells family: they were her
research paper, her doctorate, her area of specializa-
tion. She knew, for instance, that the brother with the
sallow face came from Bridgeport because one afternoon as she and Tony were leaving she saw him picked
up by a woman driving a car that had a Bridgeport
Chamber of Commerce sticker on the window; and he
had at least one child, because an infant car seat was

in the back. And Stacy and her husband must live in Newark because when he finished the *New York Times* one day, she saw him shift to the *Newark Ledger*. And Donna, who carried smelling salts, lived in Peekskill because on one sweltering day as Lydia stood in the hall, she heard Donna tell Maureen to stop complaining. "You may think anything above the Bronx line is heaven," her censorious voice said, "but let me tell you, our little hot box in Peekskill was murder, too, last night. When I went up to check on the kids at eleven, both of them were bathed in sweat." And a visit to the ladies' room on the second floor was her source for the fact that Maureen and Amy lived in New York, and Emmy Lou, who was the redhead, in Paterson, New Jersey. She was in one of the stalls just before lunch one day when she heard a familiar voice say, "Tell the truth, Emmy Lou, wasn't it a pain to pick me up this morning, that murderous Third Avenue traffic?" and the other voice she had never heard said, "Hell, no, I wouldn't want to face these Long Island highways alone, I'd even swing down to Chelsea if Amy would let us," and Maureen said, "You know Amy, a pushover for subways and buses," and Emmy Lou said, "Thank God there are no subways in Paterson or I'd—" She'd what? At this point Lydia came out and they froze. Maureen had been putting lipstick on the diminutive mouth, and Emmy Lou was teasing a wad of red hair, and both stood with hands arrested as their faces automatically shifted. Their response to the enemy: silent salvos of rancor directed into the mottled mirror of the second-floor ladies' room.

Except, as it happened, it was not a hundred-percent response. Not quite one hundred percent. Tony said he had to make a phone call when they were leaving that afternoon—did she mind waiting five minutes here in the lobby? Five minutes—well, sure. She walked over to the newspaper stand, but as she approached, she saw the distinctive blue and white stripes on the seersucker suit of Stacy's square-faced husband. Did he also see her? Probably not—he was absorbed in the headlines.

She didn't go over. Craven, she knew. She wanted a newspaper, not just for now, but also to read in the car; she loved Tony, but after a day on trial, what she wanted most was an excuse not to talk to anyone. But she couldn't face another bolt of hate. Even though she knew she functioned merely as a surrogate, the idea of his turning as she laid her change on the pile of papers and giving her close up the kind of look she had met in the ladies' room mirror made her feel suddenly sick. She went into the coffee shop at the rear of the lobby and ordered a glass of orange juice and thought about the day. On balance, not too bad. Clay hadn't sprung anything surprising, indeed, he had been surprised when the man who claimed to have seen the green car with the license number beginning with 29 emerge from the parking lot could not, on questioning, pin down the time when he saw it. Fact was, it was not a good night for him because he'd just got the news that the restaurant where he'd been a waiter for eighteen months was closing. That was the trouble with those flashy places. A big burst of popularity, everyone fighting to get in, and then the slow fizzle. So he didn't feel too hot. Did he notice that car before or after he went to his friend's house and found him not in and then had a couple of beers at that place on Linden? He couldn't rightfully remember. Sometime after ten, he knew that. Before eleven? Before twelve? Before one? Let's say somewhere around then.

And though it was not a crucial point, though the sight of the car was more important than the time of its sighting, vagueness in any aspect of a case unsettles a jury, to their suggestible minds connotes a vagueness that may slip over to other aspects as well.

So she contentedly sucked the ice from the bottom of the glass, and noted the sign—SOUP OF THE DAY, VICHYS-SOISE, $3.50—handwritten in flashy red letters and hanging lopsided on the wall, and she found it only mildly peculiar when someone took the seat beside her, although on the S-shaped counter beyond more than half the seats were empty. Then she saw the blue and white striped sleeve.

He spoke fast, out of the side of his toothy mouth. "Just thought I'd tell you," Stacy's husband said. "No matter what terrible things seem to go on, they're good people underneath. I mean, they're basically decent, they would never harm anyone—believe me, I know. Keep it in mind." Then, having dislodged the cream pitcher, he was gone. He moved fast, for someone of so stolid a build.

She turned around, she could not resist turning around, and through the glass door she saw him walk to the center of the lobby, where Stacy came out from somewhere to join him, and they walked out of sight. And two things struck her. One was that he had seen her when she stood indecisively near the newsstand; he saw her and came in specifically to deliver his kindly message. And the other was that Stacy was not meant to know about this kindliness, which came as a sweet relief after the incivility of the others. They might be the most devoted couple, he and his stout, pretty wife, but in this particular instance, he was a man operating strictly on his own.

EIGHT

LYDIA STARTED HER CASE the next morning, and Jerry was as good as she'd expected: easy but not glib, pleasant but not cloying, modest without sounding abject. All in all, a disarming witness as she led him step by step through the saga of March 24. She particularly lingered on the subject of the car. "So you told Miss Eaton your car wasn't working when in fact there was nothing wrong with it, Mr. Eldstrom? And you also gave misleading testimony to the police? You told them your car was broken though you had driven it to work that morning?" He put back his shoulders. It was a dumb mistake, his rueful voice said. Rueful but manly. He should have told Fern the truth. It was not being willing to admit to shortages in the cash department. False pride, he realizes now. Much better to have been honest. And having made up a story for Fern, he saw no way out except to keep it up for the police. Stupid: he shook a regretful head.

After all that, she watched the way he handled Clay's cross-examination. She was entitled to be proud: she'd prepared him well. What about the relationship between him and Miss Eaton? Wasn't it a fact that Miss Eaton was so in love that she would lie for him? How well did he know that high school parking lot? Hadn't he taken girls there when he was still in high school? Wasn't he the only one to have

keys to his car? . . . She'd anticipated all the areas and
had Jerry braced for them. So she felt confident when
they moved on to her character witnesses.

They all came through: Chipper, the oldest salesman, a couple of the younger ones, Mr. Neils, all pre-
senting the same message of sweetness, goodness,
consideration, reliability. She even had a surprise witness; surprising in that the man had volunteered himself. Your dream: that someone will come along and
say what needs saying. What needed saying now was
that Pam was not the only one on whom Jerry had
bent that amiable solicitude.

The new witness was a man in his fifties, and he said
if not for Jerry Eldstrom, he'd never have been able to
cope. That was the God's honest truth. Because after
twenty-five years of apartment living, he and his wife
didn't know the first thing about a house. Babes in the
wood, except the wood was a two-story affair with
green shutters and red window boxes. Weird, he had
to admit. Everyone else their age was moving out of
houses into apartments, but here they are going the
other way because Doris has emphysema, and the
doctor said maybe all those New York City fumes . . .
Well, they don't have to hear about that. But this
house they bought—it looked like such a piece of cake
when the real estate agent showed them through. It
still could be a piece of cake, he guesses, for someone
who knew his way around a tool box. First it was little things. A knocking radiator. A misfit screen. A
broken stove knob. A squeaking door. Little things,
but they add up. After a while, you get paranoid, you

think the house has it in for you and is plotting to get you out. The house is a monster who hates you.

But then you latch on to this helpful man in the hardware store. Someone who actually takes time to listen. He doesn't just sell you something and goodbye. He tells you how to use it and what to watch out for and come back tomorrow and tell him if it didn't work.

The man settled himself in the chair. "One day I went in and asked for this waterproof sealer. I heard about it on television. Miracle stuff. Spread it on and an end to water damage. So there I am ready to fork over twenty bucks—anyone else would have taken it and good riddance. But not Jerry. He says, 'Where's your leak, Mr. Selwyn?' and I tell him the basement, and he says 'What part of the basement?' and I say, 'Funny, water only comes in this one wall,' and he says, 'Now let's see what could be different about that wall.' And all this time three other people are standing there waiting. And we chew the fat a little about that one wall, and he says, 'Mr. Selwyn, you'd be throwing out your money.' Get that. I'm holding my twenty dollars for a couple of cans of this stuff they said on TV was so great, and a hardware store salesman tells me I'm throwing out my money."

Clay tried valiantly. Did they really have to hear all this? But Lydia explained that she thought it important to emphasize that it was not just to a young girl like Pam that Jerry had given that concerned attention, and the judge agreed, and Mr. Selwyn was allowed to finish his story. The incline behind the leaking wall shelved with heavy boards, and new bushes put in, and the erosion stopped, and no more leaks. An exercise in creative salesmanship. "And Jerry didn't even get a nickel out of it because Neils' doesn't sell bushes or even boards, but believe me, if Doris or I ever need anything again, we know what store we'll head for."

Mrs. Forbes was the last character witness. Self-important, kindly, nursing her bad leg, she started off at ten one morning. There was a strain of garrulousness in the woman—the inevitable garrulousness of one presented after all the hours of solitude with an audience—and Lydia had taken pains to coach her. "Don't say anything about how Jerry used to fix things in the house," she had cautioned, "because the prosecutor may ask how good a job he did, and you'll have to tell the truth, that the pipes still leaked after Jerry worked on them, and that show of incompetence might just turn someone in the jury off. Just stick to the kind of person he is. What you told me. So responsible. Such pleasant company. Such a comfort to have around the house." And it went off all right. Mrs. Forbes kept to the script.

And what could Clay say to counteract it? How gainsay this elderly woman whose life was better all around because three years ago she had rented out her second floor to Jerry Eldstrom? As she nicely put it, How lucky can you be? To find a tenant like that. Someone who gets out the shovel the moment it stops snowing so you won't break your neck on those front steps, who carries in your groceries even when your leg isn't hurting, who keeps a fifteen-year-old grand-daughter safe when the house is empty. And also, she went on grandly, someone who she has proof absolutely would not rape a girl.

"Proof, Mrs. Forbes?"

"I call it proof. Because the walls of my house—like paper. You can hear everything. And whenever he brought a girl to his room, it was quiet up there. Believe me, if there'd been any protest at all, anything unpleasant like what happened to that poor girl in the parking lot, you can bet I'd have heard."

Lydia jolted forward. This is what she can never explain to Grace. You can do all the preparation, work with the witnesses, warn of the pitfalls, ask only questions to which you know the answers. And still there it is: the unexpected slip. Sometimes it's a tidbit that will work to your advantage, and cagy, breathless, you jump in to exploit it. And sometimes it's a plum that will help the prosecution, and you pray that the prosecutor, standing slightly hunched over next to the witness stand, will not spot it.

Clay spotted it. "Did he bring many girls, Mrs. Forbes?"

"Oh, yes. Plenty. I never did keep track. But sometimes if I'd be in the kitchen, he'd bring someone in and we'd have a little chat. Always nice girls. Excuse me, young women, that's what we're supposed to call them these days. Girls who knew how to talk to someone older. Their names? Well, there was a Samantha, and a Claire, I remember her especially because I was baking an upside-down cake and Claire said her grandmother used to bake them and we talked about it."

Mrs. Forbes cast her beaming gaze around the courtroom. She had never been on a witness stand before, never expected to be, and here she was following orders exactly: being careful not to say what Miss Ness had warned her against saying, which was the fact that after Jerry fixed her pipes, they were then in worse shape than ever. But there were plenty of other nice things to bring out, she could sit here all morning keeping them interested. All these people listening, while she painted that favorable picture of her pleasant and responsible tenant.

"And let's see, there was a Margie, I seem to remember that. Or was it Margaret? And that thin one with the straight black hair on Thanksgiving. He said she was from out of town, you couldn't let a girl be without company on Thanksgiving."

"How did you feel about this, Mrs. Forbes? A young man bringing women to the apartment above you?"

"Like I said, never anything unpleasant, or I'd surely have heard."

"So you had no objection?"

"It beats going to those motels, doesn't it?"

A laugh through the courtroom. A laugh that was passed over by those in the front row, and also, Lydia saw, by Fern, who was sitting in the second row awaiting her turn. Well, God knows Fern would not laugh. As Jerry's girl friend, she had wanted to attend the trial, and Lydia had asked the judge to make an exception to the general rule that witnesses are excluded. But look what happened. Look how she had muffed it. Because it was no way to hear one's man was unfaithful, in a courtroom surrounded by a hundred strangers. The news about the car deception had been bad enough, but Fern could convince herself that there was no real guilt: a shortage of cash does not necessarily mean simply a lapse into infidelity. But sitting here in her navy dress with the white collar and cuffs, the girl had been hit with it. Samantha, Claire, Margie or was it Margaret, a nameless thin one. Girls with small talk, opinions about how to make upsidedown cake, a need for solace on Thanksgiving.

As for herself, Lydia, she felt a spasm of annoyance. One or two dates, Jerry had said, but this was more, lots more. The fact was, thanks to something heartfelt and maternal in Mrs. Forbes's approval, her testimony when balanced might not work against him. Just possibly, the jury would weigh thoughts of licentiousness against the obvious fact that with plenty of women eager to jump into bed with him, Jerry didn't need to rape someone for his sex. But he should have come clean with her. After all her warnings about openness and full communication, he should have given her that chance to work on **it, c**ertainly to prepare Fern, possibly to introduce it herself.

"Funny," she had said to Tony as they drove here one morning. "With my Legal Aid clients, the more I had to do with them, the more I liked them. There was always some redeeming feature. Some quirk or talent, or maybe just the unabashed cynicism with which they regarded the world. Why wouldn't they be cynical? The world, by and large, hadn't done them any favors. Oh, I knew they were no angels. They never pretended to be. There was no fake piety. They made it perfectly clear, most of them, that after I got them off, they were going to go right back doing whatever it was I got them off for. But this fellow, I don't know. The more we're together, the more I have reservations. It's nothing as definite as dislike—how can you not like someone so pleasant? But there's a kind of misgiving. I have the feeling he's holding out on me. Little things, like the car, but they matter. And yet I don't think he killed her. I honestly cannot imagine Jerry Eldstrom having killed that girl.''

Nothing that had gone on during the past couple of days made her revise that judgment. Just the opposite. Even the business with his parents, who in a sense could be considered an extension of him. Both of you come so the jury can see you, she had said, and yet day after day there was just one of them to demonstrate caring parenthood for the defendant. And now, of course, those girls. An affront to her and a slap in the face to Fern.

Suddenly Lydia remembered how she felt after Owen told her he was in love with that cute Marcy. There was no consoling moment of disbelief, no interval when she knew only a ladylike numbness. One instant she was an untroubled wife; the next she was a witch, venomous, mean-spirited, spiteful. She asked Owen to have the decency to leave the house, leave her alone, and before the front door slammed she was plotting measures of revenge. She would cut up into small pieces every beautiful sweater she ever gave him as a gift. She would tell the men in their natty purple uniforms who drove his limousines how they could get better wages elsewhere. She would make sure he never saw his child. She would manipulate a settlement that left him penniless. Owen never knew about these resolves, which a few days—a few hours—of reflection had been enough to soften up. But during the interval, if she saw him drowning, she would not have, she thought, lifted a finger to save him.

Fern could be a witch now, as she walked up to the witness stand. She could be feeling the spitefulness rising within her. She could reflect on the testimony she had rehearsed with shy pride and sweet assurance on that first visit from Lydia, and conclude that it was entirely up to her to decide whether or not to deliver it. She could think that if she didn't want at this moment to save a man, there was no way anyone could make her. Lydia wouldn't blame her for thinking this. No one who knew the facts would blame her.

Fern didn't look at that man as she walked through the courtroom. She circled the table where he was sitting, and went with firm steps to the chair, and smoothed down her dress—the dress whose demure aspects she and Miss Ness had also talked about—as she sat down. Her voice was steady when she gave her name; it was her own voice Lydia felt trembling. Did Fern remember the night of March 24, and would she tell the court what had happened then?

Fern looked out at the courtroom. "I do remember," she said. "It was a Tuesday. Jerry always came on Tuesdays. We usually went to a restaurant, but this night he said the car was broken, so we decided to stay home. My roommate and I had made a casserole over the weekend—eggplant and tomato and cheese. And plenty was left, so we ate that. Is that what you want to "know?" Her hooded gaze met Lydia's inquiring one.

"Do you remember what time Mr. Eldstrom left, Miss Eaton?"

She remembered that too. It was twelve on the dot. They were both tired, he'd meant to leave earlier, but they started watching this program, a funny talk show. But as soon as it was over, he put on his jacket and left.

Lydia looked over at the jury. They were listening, but not with any special alertness. The postman cradled his chin on his hand in the pose of one determined not to fall asleep, the nurse made a languid inspection of her nails, the accountant pulled at an earring. They knew there was nothing to be alert for; if the defense attorney introduced a witness who was to give the defendant his alibi, that witness was sure to be a boringly dependable one.

Clay, however, knew better. Clay, who had had the great good luck to stumble on certain facts about Jerry, knew perfectly well how undependable the knowledge of these facts could make his girl friend. Coming up for cross-examination, he started in his quiet, conversational tone. "Miss Eaton, you say you remember where you were on the night of March twenty-fourth?" ("Please speak up, Miss Eaton," the judge said.) "Well, then, do you remember where you were on the night of March twenty-third?"

"I suppose I was working. I usually work on Mondays."

"So the only reason you remember March twenty-third is because of the work schedule you adhere to."

"I guess so. Yes."

"Where do you work, Miss Eaton?"

"At the Sea and Spray Health Club."

"I see. And how rigid is the scheduling at the club?"

Fern wet her lips. If the other receptionist, Lorna, was sick, or if there was some special event like a party, they changed things around.

"Does that happen often?"

"Not very often."

"So you conclude that because March twenty-third was a Monday, you must have been at work."

"That's right."

"And by the same token, because March twenty-fourth was a Tuesday, you think you must have seen Mr. Eldstrom."

"Yes. I mean yes." ("Please speak up, Miss Eaton," the judge had said again.)

"Suppose I were to tell you that one week before the twenty-fourth and twenty-third, that is, on the seventeenth and sixteenth of March, you worked at the club on a Tuesday and were free on Monday."

"If you say so."

"The club records say so, Miss Eaton. I have them here—I'd like to introduce them at this time." And when the technicalities attending this were finished, "I take it, Miss Eaton, you don't remember that particular switch in work time."

"Not exactly."

"But if your whereabouts on those two days aren't fresh in your recollection, how is it you remember so well where you were just one week later?"

Lydia watched her. Oh, Fern, how I wish I could help you. If Jerry had played fair with me, I could have prepared you better, you wouldn't be in a state of shock while having to deal with this inquisition.

"Miss Eaton, I suggest there's a reason you specifically remember the night of March twenty-fourth. I suggest that Mr. Eldstrom called you and told you how important it would be for you to remember it. Isn't that the case?"

Fern chewed on the inside of her cheek. "He did call and say he was in trouble about that murder."

"Ah. And didn't he also tell you that his alibi depended on your saying that he was with you for that evening?"

"He said something like that. I don't remember the exact words."

"Miss Eaton, didn't he say words to the effect that you were his girl, his only girl, and he counted on you?"

"I guess so."

"Miss Eaton, you found out three days ago in this court that Mr. Eldstrom's statement about his car was incorrect. That it was not a need for repair but a desire for economy that kept him from driving on that particular night. Today you found out something else pertaining to your relationship with Mr. Eldstrom. So my question, Miss Eaton, is this: does it change your recollection about March twenty-fourth to learn, as you have this morning, that you were not in fact Mr. Eldstrom's only girl?"

Well, here they were. The eye of the storm. The heart of the matter. The bull's-eye at the center of the target. The nurse was no longer studying her nails, the accountant had given up the tug at an earring, the postman sat alert; along with everyone else in the courtroom, they recognized that Clay had got to where he was heading all along. As for Fern, she was very quiet. The hand that had been plucking at the white collar dropped into her lap; the gaze that had been fixed, mesmerized, on Clay, went out to the back of the courtroom. But her voice was steady. "It wouldn't change anything because Jerry was with me that night. It was just like I said. He came around eight, and we ate that leftover casserole because he said the car was broken, and he left at twelve o'clock. And I know it was March twenty-fourth. I really do know it. I remember exactly."

Her head went up as she uttered the last triumphant words—the health club would be proud of her, Lydia thought. I'm proud of her. And what of Jerry, that amiable spirit with his penchant for small fibs and petty betrayals—would he ever prevail on her to spend an evening from eight to twelve with him again? Would he win the valiant Miss Eaton back? Was he worthy of winning her back? Lydia packed her papers into her briefcase, and she and Tony went down for lunch.

NINE

"SO WHAT DO YOU THINK?" Tony asked when the waitress had brought their sandwiches.

Their unpalatable sandwiches. She'd have preferred staying in the courthouse coffee shop, where the service was slow and the noise level horrendous but at least the food was edible, but she also did not care to meet any of the Howells family, whom she had seen going in there from time to time. She didn't even care to meet Stacy's husband, whose stony face when she stood next to him in the elevator this morning made clear that his foray into kindliness was not to be presumed on.

So here they were in the Arden Restaurant, two blocks from the courthouse, and Tony, understandably, was anxious to talk over the events of the morning.

"What do I think about Jerry? I want to wring his neck." She bit into a tasteless tomato. "No, I'll amend that. I want to get him off. Then I'd like to wring his neck."

Actually, when the court recessed, Jerry was someone else anxious to talk over events of the morning. Their quick exchange at the table didn't satisfy him, she knew that; he'd have liked to sit down with her so he could explain and justify and extenuate. And he would have extenuations, that facile Jerry: a story to explain it all. Samantha in his version might be a friend of the family whose father had asked him to be nice to her, and Claire would be someone he went to high school with who happened to be in town for just two weeks, and Margie/Margaret, well, she might emerge as the girl friend of another salesman at Neils' who came to Jerry for friendly consultation when her own affair was getting rocky, and as for the Thanksgiving waif, in his earnest portrayal she would be so frail, so unprepossessing, as not to be compared with a girl as bountifully supplied with attractiveness as Fern. And what Mrs. Forbes with her prurient imagination didn't realize, none of them were in a position to entertain him in rooms of their own, which was the reason, the only reason, he invited them to his place. Listening to all this, his mother, who was the parent present today, would nod in judicious agreement, and after a while Lydia would find herself sliding into credulity as well. It could be true. Jerry's explanations could all be true. The only thing was, right at the moment she didn't want to hear them. She had enough on her mind.

One of the things on her mind was the summation. Her already-prepared summation that in view of this morning's disclosures might have to be subtly altered. "Will this make things harder?" Tony had asked. "Now that he looks like such a shit, will it be harder?" Well, it might be a little harder, but as she sat here, forcing herself to take another bite so she would have energy for this afternoon, the new words emerged full-blown in her mind.

"Jerry Eldstrom is not a saint, ladies and gentlemen. He's a young man who likes a good time. And his idea of a good time is to go out with girls. Not just one girl. He's happy if he sees one girl one week, and another the next, and still another the third. But"—her voice rising with the solemn weight of its message—"but he is not a murderer, ladies and gentlemen. Not remotely a murderer or a rapist. There is no compelling evidence linking Jerry Eldstrom to that terrible crime, and there is nothing in his makeup that would allow him to commit it."

The summations were scheduled for the day after tomorrow—court would be recessed tomorrow for the Fourth. So all that had to be encountered first was the Mrs. Lateen whom Clay had promised for rebuttal. To rebut what? Lydia and Tony wondered. Jerry had said he didn't know her. The name—Ida Lateen—didn't ring a bell. Now Tony finished his last bite of sandwich—ah, youth, to be able to eat anything—and said he had an idea. He had been out to interview this Mrs. Lateen, but all she'd said was I'll talk to you from the witness stand. But let's suppose she was the exception, he said. The one customer out of four years of unremitting amiability whom Jerry had offended. She stood waiting one day while he bent his endless patience on Mr. Selwyn or someone like him, and after fifteen minutes she blew up, and Jerry insulted her. Or, wait. Better still, she purchased six screws and then brought them back for an exchange, and then did it again, and when she showed up a third time, Jerry lost his temper. It had been a hard day, and the perfect Jerry lost his temper. "Listen, you old bag," he said,

"I can't be changing six lousy screws for you for-ever."

Tony interrupted the fantasy to tell the waitress he wanted chocolate layer cake for dessert. "No, he didn't say 'you old bag,' but his face said it. And she got furious, imagine treating Ida Lateen like that, and she said she'd tell his boss, at which point Jerry said—Let's see. Jerry said, 'You do that and you'll wish to God you never set foot in this store.' Which I suppose could be construed as a threat. So it's the contention of the prosecution that this negates all the bouquets that have been tossed at Jerry's character so far be-cause someone who could make so virulent a threat to a customer could also take a girl to a deserted parking lot and kill her."

Lydia laughed. It was a help to laugh. She said it sounded a little far-fetched, but it could well be some-thing like that. Certainly the clips they had on Mrs. Lateen made it seem possible. She was one of those women who are a staple of every community—per-forming good works while amassing ill will. Tony had gone through past issues of the *North Rainey Daily Times* for a decade, and the headlines were there. IDA LATEEN IN FAVOR OF EARLIER CLOSING TIME FOR RED BARON RESTAURANT. TOO MUCH NOISE FROM YOUTH REC HALL: IDA LATEEN. MRS. LATEEN RAPS NEW NEON LIGHTING ON MAIN STREET. BIKE RACING ON SUNDAY MORNING MUST STOP, SAYS MRS. LATEEN. She had lived in North Rainey for fifty-two years and occu-pied herself with its activities for almost as long. "I love this town," she said in an interview, but it might be held debatable whether the affection was recipro-

cated; she had twice lost an election for the honorary
job of mayor.

It was two-fifteen when this exemplar of civic responsibility took her place on the witness stand. This
was no Mrs. Forbes, thrilled at finding herself with so
many nice people to talk to. Mrs. Lateen sat with the
air of one accustomed to coercing audiences into
sharing her opinion; as her clarion voice took the oath,
she made clear she was prepared to offer censure and
edification in equal measure. But censure and edification about what? Despite the compelling range of
Tony's imagination, Lydia still was puzzled.

What Mrs. Lateen said, in answer to Clay's
methodical questioning, was that she saw Jerry Eldstrom get out of his car on the night of March twenty-
fourth. It was late. Late by her standards, anyhow.
Eleven-thirty. She knows the time because she was at
a meeting to discuss an ordinance that would forbid
people to start mowing their lawns before seven
A.M.She realizes that may sound like a petty issue, but
when you think of the many elderly people who need
their sleep... No, she knows that's not pertinent. My
error, Your Honor. She just wants to establish that
she's making no mistake about the time. Because Tilly
Hayes, who was chairman, had said, "Look at this,
quarter past eleven, that ties it," and it takes her fifteen minutes exactly to drive home from the library,
where they have their meetings in that downstairs
room. Anyhow, as she slowed down to make the turn
into her driveway, she noticed a man getting out of a
car just in front. An old green car; she specifically
noted a beat-up fender. Yes, as it happens she did see

the license plate. Or at least the first two numbers. Two and nine, same as had been assigned to the green murder car. She also looked at the man. She looked at him carefully, because Harry has been dead these seven years, and when you're a woman driving alone into a garage late at night, well, in this day and age, she doesn't have to elaborate. Just common sense to keep your eyes open. No, she must admit, the man did not turn around. But she saw his profile. She also saw what he was wearing: chino pants and a green jacket, which she has seen many times on the defendant, who lives with or, should she say, rents a room from Mrs. Forbes just a block and a half from her house. And she saw the way he was built and also the way he walked. The same precise walk as the defendant. That little tilt to the left. She waited till he got to the corner. Then she turned into her driveway and the electric eye opened the door to her garage and she drove in.

She was impressive, Lydia thought. Not ingratiating, God knows not attractive, but impressive. That officious voice uttering "eleven-thirty"—a rebuttal, all right—when Jerry and Fern had both made a point of that twelve o'clock departure time. At least, she impressed the jury. By now, Lydia was a speed reader of the minute changes in their posture: the lips curled in reluctant assent, the rueful heaves of shoulder, the small nods as if in ratification of each incriminating detail. And of course she saw the gloating on the front-row faces. Donna held the perennial package of mints aloft. This was more like it: at last a plus for their side.

Lydia went up to the judge. Not quite three o'clock, she pointed out. She could easily finish her cross-examination by four. Could they have a half-hour recess?

"Is it important?"

"Very, Your Honor."

She got the time, and she and Tony repaired to a small room off the judge's chambers. "Okay, let's see all the stuff on that woman. You do this pile, I'll do this one." It didn't take long. She wished they had more time, but if you know what you're looking for, it sometimes jumps out at you. Before the half hour was up, she was back, hair combed, lipstick freshened, argument ready.

It started like any cross-examination in which an attorney seeks to shake an assertion of identity. How bright were the streetlights when the witness saw this male figure? How did he differ from dozens of other men who in spring wear green jackets and chino pants? Could she be sure, in that dim illumination, of the color of the other car? Does she make a practice of noting the numbers on licenses? Did she have her own car lights on when she saw what she claims was Jerry's profile? All very cut and dried. From the jury box, stifled yawns and a renewed attention to nails.

Then Lydia moved a step away. "Mrs. Lateen, I understand you're very active in North Rainey civic matters."

"Oh, I surely am." A proud shake of the coiffured head.

"One subject in which you've shown an interest is housing."

It surely was.

"If I'm correct, at various meetings last year and the year before, you took a vigorous position on this matter. You objected to the practice by which homeowners in North Rainey rent out part of their homes. The kind of arrangement, that is, that allows Mrs. Forbes to rent her top floor to Mr. Eldstrom."

Clay predictably objected, the judge overruled, and Mrs. Lateen explained that she certainly did object to such rentals.

"Could you tell the court the nature of your objection?"

Easily. She thought renting out a part of someone's house diminished real estate values, put an unfair burden on those taxpayers who did not resort to such expediences, added noise and traffic to already congested streets. In short, it was a practice to downgrade the neighborhood.

Lydia picked up a pile of what were obviously newspaper clippings, and waving them conspicuously, she walked in front of the jury. "By the way, Mrs. Lateen, isn't it a fact that you introduced a resolution in the city council outlawing such rentals?"

Mrs. Lateen was proud to have been the author of this resolution.

"And do you remember how the council voted?"

Mrs. Lateen remembered very well. Because of a protest by some misguided people, the resolution lost by a two-to-one margin. She was sorry about that. She thought it constituted a real blow to the stability and dignity of a distinguished residential community.

Lydia paused for a minute. The jury was leaning forward again; people who might want to rent out attics, store-rooms, basements, unused wings in their houses, or, conversely, find accommodations themselves in such habitable quarters. A jury of one's peers: this is what is meant. "Am I also right, Mrs. Lateen, in thinking that another subject in which you've expressed an interest is the matter of overnight parking on residential streets?"

Lydia was right.

"Here, too, I think you took a strong position. At a meeting just six months ago, you introduced a bill to prohibit parking between one A.M. and five A.M. on the streets of certain designated areas."

She assuredly did that.

"In other words, it's your position, Mrs. Lateen, that overnight parking in these neighborhoods be restricted to people who own their own garages."

That was correct.

"I'm going to read a statement you're quoted by the *North Rainey Daily Times* as having made."

"Your Honor, is this necessary?" Clay.

His Honor thought it was, and Lydia went on. "'Letting those people who don't have their own garages and thus are not bona fide residents park overnight does more than simply clutter up our streets. It introduces an undesirable element into our neighborhoods. While respectable citizens sleep, who knows what thieves, what muggers, what other sort of criminals, may be lurking outside our very windows night after night. These people are invited in by our misjudgment and kept here by our negligence. It is time to reassess our policies.' Did you in fact say this, Mrs. Lateen?''

She had said it.

''As a matter of fact, Mrs. Lateen, isn't it a fair statement of your convictions that you think someone who comes home late at night is more likely to be a rapist or a murderer than someone who keeps more normal hours?''

Mrs. Lateen said that was a fair statement.

''It follows then, does it not, that if Mr. Eldstrom should be convicted of murder, this verdict would go far toward bolstering your contention about undesirable elements?''

Well, this was not allowed. Lydia hardly expected that it would be. Behind her, she realized there was another silence. The silence of fervent attention. Should she try another question? Go at it obliquely? Could she be sure the jury got the point, that Mrs. Lateen had a vested interest in identifying the man who walked in front of her on March 24 as Jerry Eldstrom?

Then the woman on the stand leaned forward. Her hands waved, the angry red color that had tinged her cheeks crept up to her hairline. ''Listen here,'' she said, and it was clear that this was no Fern trying to contain her wounded feelings within a seemly show of dignity. Not even an expansive Mrs. Forbes enjoying her day in the sun. ''They're no good, not one of them. This man, if he didn't murder that poor girl, he'll get to someone else. They're interlopers, those people. They have no right in our community. They don't belong here. They're not the element we want. If we had any sense, we'd put them out, all of them.''

''That will be all. Thank you, Mrs. Lateen.''

TEN

I WAS TOO HAPPY, is what she thought after it happened. I should have known. You can't let yourself be lulled into purest happiness. You have to keep reminding yourself, before fate takes over the job, of the possibilities for disaster: the beam that may fall, the cable that may snap, the brakes that are unable to mesh on time. Life.

She was purely happy when she went to pick up Addie at nursery school. From the sheer force of joy, she seemed to be detached from herself, a disembodied spirit of benignity, at the same time as she could envision herself: a pretty woman in a blue silk suit walking fast at six-fifteen on a July evening even though heat still rises from the city street and not a breeze is stirring. Walking fast and counting to herself the tally of her pleasures. The look of sly relief on the face of the black housewife when it turned out Mrs. Lateen was a monster of snobbish exclusivity. The sign with which the physical education teacher and the accountant greeted the same development. The overt grin on the perky face of the telephone repair woman. Indeed, the collective exhalation of breath from all of them, those twelve good people, on having the traducer of Jerry show her true colors.

And of course the praise from Ben, when she and Tony got back to the office. "You did it. Set the trial back on course."

"I was lucky."

"Lydia, don't give me that. Luck in courtrooms doesn't just happen. You have to set the stage for it, give it a nudge, coax it in. So go home, enjoy your holiday."

"Listen, the trial's not over yet."

"It might as well be."

She didn't argue. Ben had it right. The day after tomorrow, she thought, the jury will do what they give every indication of desiring to do, which is to vote for acquittal. "Remember, your duty is to withhold your final judgment till you've heard all the evidence and also the instructions given by the court. That will be one of your hardest jobs: to wait till you've heard it all." So the judge had instructed them at the beginning. But they aren't waiting. Without having heard the summations or the judge's charge, they have made up their minds.

As for those brooding people in the front row, they will be heartsick, indeed, they are heartsick already: they can read the signs as well as she can. But they will have to bear it. The wrongful conviction of a young man would not have returned their girl to them—little by little they will understand. And after understanding will come resignation, and after that—God knows they're entitled to it—comfort.

Meanwhile the court was recessed for July Fourth, which this year came on a Wednesday. Not so good for some people, perhaps, as a Monday or Friday, but bliss for her, giving her a respite when she needs it and a day with Addie when she longs for it. Even the city looked golden, that hour when people usually drag themselves from office to bus and subway but today walk with festive tread as if allied in a promise to Lydia Ness that tomorrow will be fine, tomorrow will present the happiness she has earned and the luck she has set the stage for.

So the woman in her silk suit hugged her mistaken assumptions as she rang the bell at the nursery school. Diane would answer it. When Lydia called at five to say sorry, she knows it's hard on them, but she'll have to be fifteen minutes late again tonight, Melanie said Diane was the one who would probably stay over. And Lydia was not to worry. Tonight, as it happens, she's not the only late one. Sadie Lee's mother also phoned that she was held up, and so did Peter's. Diane was probably soothing Peter, Lydia thought when the bell wasn't answered promptly. As a child with a high IQ and a low emotional breaking point, Peter had been known to react in drastic ways to being overtired. Screaming, throwing toys, even biting. He may be biting now, his pearly teeth leaving their pink indentations on Sadie Lee's tender arm, or Addie's—no wonder Diane can't immediately come.

Diane came. She opened the door and promptly left it.

"On the phone," her cracked voice said. "Calling them! Police! Addie!"

Lydia followed into the adjoining room, where the phone was on a hook too high for small arms to reach. In her high school days, a favorite set piece of the biology teacher was an exposition about the teeming species of life suspended in a single drop of water, and now she was conscious of the manifold ideas that could be suspended in a single instant; simultaneously, that is, a woman can view the neat array of blocks on a shelf of the toddler room, and see into each empty corner of the room for three-year-olds, and take in the distortions of Diane's face as she stands holding the phone, and also understand in the very depths of her soul that the worst thing in the world has happened.

"No!" she shrieked. "No!"

"Lydia, hush. I'm calling the police, they'll come, they always—"

"Yes. Call them. Call!" The emptiness spread like a blight through her whole body; when she swayed, she felt her head hit something hard. The walls rocked, a revolving procession of small cabinets, children's clothing, drawings, toys that offered the exquisite peace of vertigo—at the same instant, a corner of her mind told her that such solace was out of the question. She opened her eyes; with an effort, she held them open. "God help me," she murmured.

"Lydia, I hear them now."

She squinted, trying to make sense of Diane's figure leaning above her: the heavy cheeks, the course, dark hair, the scowling eyes; but what she saw, what stubborn vision insistently gave her, was a sign hanging lopsided on a wall. SOUP OF THE DAY, it said. VICHYSSOISE, $3.50 Why soup? Why the flashy red handwritten letters? Then she understood.

She reached up for the phone. "Give it to me."

"Just sit there, I'll do it. Police? They're here now. Police?"

Lydia's finger managed to take possession of the receiver. "It's all right, operator," she told that voice trained for impersonal helpfulness at the other end. "A mistake. Nothing wrong."

"Nothing wrong!" Diane's face seemed to fly apart.

"First tell me," Lydia said.

"But if they try now. If they come right away and get her."

Her. "Who?"

"The cleaning woman." The cracked voice had lapsed into a wail.

"Diane— No, I'm all right, I swear. I just have to hear exactly what happened. Then we can act." Lydia Ness, prodigy, all at once, of serene reasonableness. "So the sooner you tell me..."

Diane told it with interjections of sobs, of promises to kill herself, of please to be allowed back on the phone. She had been with the three children. Peter and Sadie Lee and Addie. And Peter started to throw up. One of the things that happens to him when he gets too tired. If ever there was a child who ought to be picked up on time. So she took him into the bathroom, where he heaved and heaved and got a little out. And when she wiped him off and went out— Dear God, will she ever forget that sight—only Sadie Lee was in the room, and the front door, the perpetually locked front door, was slightly ajar.

Where's Addie? she asked. No—in answer to Lydia—she didn't scream it. You don't scream with children, and at that point there was no one else to hear; a day like this, stifling, the other people in the building are out at five-thirty sharp. And Sadie Lee—she was playing with the doll house—Sadie Lee said, "Addie went to help the cleaning woman." And just then the two mothers stood at the door. Peter's and Sadie Lee's.

"Did you tell them what happened?"

"I tried to. But Peter's mother was talking. She always comes in and swoops him up, but just today, this long story. How Peter's father believes in strict discipline and she's more permissive, so they're always battling it out in front of the child, and that's why he—well, you know. On and on. I couldn't get her to cut it off."

"So you *didn't* tell them."

"No. I don't know why not. I wish I was dead."

She might not know why, but Lydia knew. Because the fundamental thing a nursery school must deliver is safety. Because it is unthinkable for a child to be lost. Because knowledge of a disaster like that spells the end of a school. And because Diane's consciousness of these absolutes superseded, for a grotesque moment, even her panic about an adored child.

"What about Sadie Lee? Did you get excited in front of her? I mean, will she think there was something wrong?"

"Don't ask me how I kept calm, but I did. A three-year-old, after all—"

"Right." So Sadie Lee isn't likely to report a catastrophe to her mother.

"Lydia!" Diane was not calm now. She had been able to handle it when Lydia dissolved, like any bereft parent, into anguished hysteria; she herself was the masterful one. But now the shift in roles had left her lost, even captious. "You hurt your head, you're still dizzy, that's why—"

"No. I feel all right."

"Then why are you asking all these questions? We're losing time. It's only ten minutes since it happened. Maybe less."

"I have another question. What's this?"

This was a folded piece of paper on the floor. She had stepped on it when she came in, one side bore the imprint of the sole of her shoe, but when she unfolded it, the words were clear. WE WANT JUSTICE,in large capital letters, spread across the entire page.

Ah. "Diane, look," she said. And when the bristling eyes turned on it a distracted glance, she folded it and put it in her pocket. Still another question, she said. Was there a cleaning woman who had a key and came in regularly?

"Well, sure. How else could we keep this place decent, day after day? Six-thirty usually, but sometimes six-fifteen is her time—if the mothers are late, I see her."

Lydia could see her, too. A woman in gray uniform? White? Gray and white? Anyhow, a woman approaching a child who has been trained, even at three years old, not to take things from strangers. Never candy, baby, you understand? Not a ride. Not a drink, even if your throat is all dried up... But no one told that amiable child not to give help. So if a woman wearing the accustomed outfit said, Honey, would you come and hold this little dustpan, if she were smart enough to make it a game.

That incensed wail was starting again. "Lydia, they can still stop it. They'll cordon off the whole area, hundreds of policemen, thousands, that's how they do it, no one can get away. Oh, God, I really will kill myself."

"Diane, shut up for a second. Please? Let me think."

Yes. What she has to do. Think which is the best way to save her child. To call the police, that act of guaranteed comfort that puts you immediately into the posture of helplessness, weakness, cosseted passivity? Or to consider seriously whom you are up against, what they want from you, what course is least likely to render them injurious? Why had she imagined it would ebb quietly away, that shifting tide of misery in the front row? The fact was, all the bustling they did— peppermints passed, and shawls arranged and rearranged, and shoelaces loosened, and collars undone—those exercises in trivia were simply an analogue for the activity that was going on someplace else: people plotting, spying, casing the territory, assessing the risks, fixing on the awful strategy in case events turned against them. Events had turned. The defense lawyer, with her adroit tactics, had turned them.

"Diane, listen. You know the case I've been on, you read the papers. There's this agonized family who are desperate for vengeance the way... well, the way anyone would be. And they're not getting it. Instead, they've lost everything. First they lost their daughter, and now they've lost her again; it's as if she's ceased to exist. I mean, the trial isn't even about her. It's about Jerry Eldstrom. How good-humored and charming and gentle he is, how the customers choose him, the girls love him. That's how they see it. They're terribly wrong, but that's their view. The trial's a cheat. And after what happened today, they're afraid they're going to be cheated out of retribution; from where they're sitting, I'm the one to cheat them.''

When she paused, her gaze wandered to the shelves where the finger paints were lined up. Last week Addie explained the finger painting she brought home. "See, that's a big dog up there, and he really likes little girls, he doesn't want to bite them.'' Addie working out her fears as she swirls the black and blue paint around with her fingers.

Maybe Diane had the same vision: a child in green coveralls, a streak of paint across her cheek. "It's not fair,'' she cried out.

"That's what those people think,'' Lydia said. "The criminal justice system has not been fair to them, and they're going to do something to amend it. They have no interest in hurting Addie.'' Go on. Say it forcefully, persuasively, as if you don't also have to convince yourself. "None at all. Why should they? They want me to give them a chance to avenge their girl's death. That's all they want.''

Words came out of Diane's distorted mouth. "This is the most insane—''

"It's true. One of them told me this would happen.''

"Lydia, what are you talking about?''

"First I thought he was just trying to be kind. Off-hand kindness to counteract their hostility. Their ir-rational, really uncivilized, hostility. But now I realize. There was nothing offhand about it at all. It was a deadly serious message. He was telling me they'd do something terrible, but if I kept cool, then things would work out all right."

The wail had risen to a scream. "You mean he told you they'd take Addie and you didn't stop it?"

She pictured him as he stood there, his square face strained, his toothy mouth barely moving, his arm in the blue and white striped seersucker jolting the pitcher of ersatz cream. "He didn't exactly tell me. Obviously. But he wanted me to keep in mind they were basically decent so I wouldn't take some rash ac-tion that would make matters worse."

Was that the case? *No matter what terrible things seem to go on, they're good people underneath.* It could be exactly what it purports to be, a message to set her straight. Remember that whatever they do, these are good people who would not allow any in-jury to a child.

But couldn't it also function as a shaky justifica-tion? Remember that whatever they do, these are good people who were pushed to the edge? No, it could not be that. Otherwise he would not have slipped away from his wife, followed Lydia into the coffee shop, bent on her a look of such pointed intensity.

"Yes, I see it all now," she said. "He was power-less to stop it—only a brother-in-law, after all—but he knew what they were planning. Because they have been planning it. All this time, they've been finding out about me. Where I live, my child, my habits, everything. Easy. Nine of them. Counting spouses, eighteen. That's without the mother and father, who are too old and feeble. My guess is they're not in on it. Besides, some of them never showed up at the trial. I wondered about that, but now I understand. It's so they'd be free to act. One of them to follow me and I wouldn't recognize him, and another maybe to case the place here, and another to bribe that cleaning woman to give up her keys, and another...another to take her home.'' Keep going. In the face of Diane's furious qualms, don't let your voice tremble. "One of their homes," she said. "In New Jersey or Connecticut or, I don't know, right here in New York. They're going to keep her till I do the right thing."

"And what's that?"

"Get Jerry Eldstrom convicted," she said.

"And how can you do that?"

"How? I can find something against him. Everyone has a black spot if you look hard enough. I can tear down that picture of sweetness and goodness I constructed and labeled Jerry Eldstrom."

"You mean, you'd go against your own client?"

"To get Addie back? Would I ever!"

Diane sat turning this over. Her mouth working, her hands pulling at the disheveled hair. Finally she jumped up. "I never heard anything so crazy. Someone has Addie, and you stand there talking about that trial. I'm going to call the police. You can't stop me."

She watched Diane go halfway across the room. A big woman who can be tender with children but now looks top-heavy, awkward. The rubbery cheeks, the coarsened nose, the eyes pinched and red from crying. "Diane, stop."

"You don't know any of this. You just don't know."

"I know for days they've been sending me a message. Oh, not with words exactly. But each time someone put a shawl on Mama. Or replied with a groan from Papa. Or put her hands over her ears to shut out the encomiums to Jerry's virtue. Each gesture a reminder of what they want."

"Don't you want to save your own child?"

Her hand reached out and pulled back. Don't slap her. It will just make it worse.

"What if they harm her? Did you ever think of that?"

When her foot shook, it brushed against something small and fragile. The couch from the doll house. The couch with brocade upholstery, graceful curved legs. "He said they wouldn't and I believe him. Besides, why should they? What good would it do? They want to put pressure on me, is all. It's very smart, actually. A brilliant tactic. They give me a day to come up with something, a day when the court doesn't function because of the Fourth. It's their way of saying when the trial resumes on Thursday morning, they expect things to be different."

"You mean"—amazing: a thin, high voice emerging from those heavy features—"you're not going to tell the police till Thursday? Your child is missing and you're going to wait until then!"

In an effort to get Diane away from the phone, she edged them both sideways, into the toddler room.

Such an array of simple, unbreakable toys—you forget how quickly the two-year-old stage changes into that surge of knowingness and competence at three. Was it just a year ago Addie used to climb the steps of the baby slide, hover shakily on top in an appeal for help, shrug off help when it was offered, and, captain of her own fate, slide valiantly, gloriously down?

"Not just me, Diane," she said. "Both of us. We're in it together."

"You really expect me to—"

"Listen. I know these people. I've spent two weeks studying them. I've paid more attention to them, I think, than to my own client. And believe me, they're decent. Something else that man said. Hurt and bitter right now, yes, but basically decent and human. They have children of their own, dozens of them. They would never purposely hurt a child, never, never."

"What if it's an accidental hurt?"

"That's exactly what I'm talking about. That risk." Talking in her controlled, lucid voice: a woman selling her case to the most resistant jury she has ever faced. "Diane, look at it this way. Let's say a family takes her home to their own children, maybe right here in New York. They make up some story about the new child and their kids accept it. They give her supper. They bathe her. They put her to sleep." Oh, God, without her yellow blanket! Her rag doll! "Well, that's one scenario. She's okay. She's sleeping. But suppose with those people who are all in constant communication, a sister who lives in New Jersey calls her New York sibling and says the police have been snooping around. Then what will that alerted family do? Will they leave the new kid in her makeshift bed? Or will they rouse her, cover her up, hustle her out of there fast? Hustle her where? That's the thought that makes my blood run cold.''

''You mean, if an alarm goes out?''

''Exactly. You can't hide an active, healthy child. A child who's playing around. So what we want is for them to have no need to hide her. To not even think about hiding her.''

''You don't want them to panic.''

''That's it, Diane. No panic.'' There! They have gotten through it without either of them saying the dread words. Dead. Killed. Murdered. Slain. Lydia and Diane, masters of the euphemistic exegesis.

''If I hadn't taken Peter into the bathroom. If I'd just let him throw up here.''

''Stop it. You did what you had to. Diane, will you play it my way? Will you?''

''I guess so.'' Diane bent down to the lowest shelf. One of the animals—a bear with a green ribbon around its middle—had tumbled sideways, and her tender fingers set it straight. When she looked up it was with a new expression. Bitter cunning. ''Did you ever think it just might be the cleaning woman? The real one. There are these gangs—criminals—that always want children. Pretty children. They sell them for adoption in other countries,'' she said, and her voice was not hysterical at all. It was filled with a cold accusatory anger, the anger of a woman being swept into something for which she feels thorough disapproval. ''Your own child in the hands of one of those gangs. Are you willing to take that kind of risk?'' she said, and the rage in her voice amounted to a kind of viciousness.

Lydia put her hand behind her, but the only thing to steady herself on was the rung of a chair designed for three-year-olds. Then she reached into her pocket. "Gangs who kidnap children don't write notes like this. Look at it, Diane. Oh, for God's sake, *really* look. WE WANT JUSTICE. I told you—what those people want and see no way of getting unless they take things into their own hands. They're crazy, but in a funny way they're also right."

Diane took a deep breath. "You're the crazy one. But of course, your child, you're the one to decide," she said in her new, cold voice. She went over to the clothes cabinet. "Here's Addie's sweater. Do you want it?"

Lydia stared. Not a sweater, actually. A sweatshirt. Pink, with a design of sequins emblazoned on the front. Owen brought it one day when the child was not quite one, and Lydia stored it in a closet for two years, and this spring, though it was still large and also unsuitable, she let Addie wear it. Now she watched as Diane folded it so the gaudy decoration was on top. If I take it, Addie will be all right. If I don't take it, Addie will be all right.

"And, Diane, another thing. You can't be crying when you go out of here. You can't even look upset. There's always someone to see everything. Who's that child who lives just two blocks away? Dolly? Dottie? Well, suppose Dottie and her mother go out for, I don't know, ice cream, and it turns out this is the way they go. So if someone meets you, can you look absolutely serene? A teacher who's just given children a rewarding day? Diane, can you?''

Maybe priests feel like this. Go out and sin no more, they tell the abject congregation, but it's the sinful feeling in their own breasts they're trying to exorcise. Will she be able to arrange on her ravaged face the look of mendacious serenity she advised for Diane? She walked out into the lobby, where she and Addie walk together every evening. Usually there's a period of—well, not quite coolness, call it rather formality, as a child struggles to make the transition from teacher to mother. By the time they hit the street, it is over. When they've gone up the three steps to the street, Addie has taken the hand Lydia is offering. Pick me up, she says; a small girl wanting to be babied but also ready to fight the appurtenances of babyhood. Lydia doesn't pick her up but she bends down and hugs her, and they both laugh.

Lydia looked down now, as if that dark, ambivalent head might materialize beside her. Her knees were shaking. If she's the one to meet Dottie and her mother, she knows exactly what will happen. Addie? she will say. You want to know why I'm leaving school and Addie isn't with me? Because a fake cleaning woman kidnapped her, that's why. And maybe I'm doing the right thing in not telling the police, and maybe, God help me, I'm not.

She didn't meet Dottie and her mother. There was no one to put those provocative questions, so she simply walked on, her heels clicking on the steaming sidewalk and the pink sweatshirt with sequins dangling from her hand.

ELEVEN

SHE WALKED TILL she reached the corner. Then, just before she waved for a taxi, doubt washed over her like a sickness. She leaned for a minute against the window of a drugstore. When news got out that she was leaving Legal Aid, Phil Monroney came up to her one day. "Hear we have to get along without you, Lydia." He had been the detective assigned to her when she felt it necessary to see the scene of a crime, or to speak to a witness who might be found only at the scene of a crime. More than a dozen times, he had shepherded her up the kind of staircase or along the kind of street where no woman wants to find herself, and each time, with him beside her, she felt, if not comfortable, at least safe. His canny instincts, his hulking presence, his aggressive calm. "If you ever need help, I'm your man," he had said in that farewell chat. She had smiled, looking into his bantering gaze—once she was working for Ben Lyttle, why in the world would she need Phil Monroney?—but now she opened her address book and turned to M. Then she went across the street to an outdoor phone.

"Phil? It's Lydia."

"Hey, girl, how you doing?"

"Phil, you once said if I needed help."

No pause at all. The only interruption came because someone tapped on the door of the booth, she had to wave him away. Where was she now? Phil wanted to know.

"I can be home in ten minutes."

"Beat you to it."

He didn't. When she came in, the lobby held only the doorman and a woman berating her dog: if the dog did not start behaving better, she wouldn't ever take him to the park again. But a minute later she heard a taxi, and Phil walked in, as big, as rumpled, as comforting as ever.

By the time the elevator reached her floor, she had told him everything. She even started to cry—the tears Diane had preempted when they were at the school. She unlocked her door and sat opposite him in the living room and wept. She doesn't know what to do. She can't live without her baby. Everything is going round and round. It had seemed the right decision when it happened, but now, how can she tell? She can't live without her baby. Even this piece of paper—maybe one of those gangs could have written it.

Phil shook his head. "Kidnap gangs don't leave messages about justice. From what you tell me, it's them, all right. That family. I know those people. The system has battered them, and they have to strike out. Action, action. Only in this case the wrong person is the fall guy."

"So what do I do? Phil, what should I do!"

"You sure nobody else knows about this so far?"

"Only Diane. The teacher. I told you."

When he crossed his legs, her spindly desk chair shifted under him. "Nine families, you say? Nine brothers and sisters? So tell me this, Lydia. Is there any way you can get their addresses? All nine of them? No matter where they live?''

Those facile tears started again. ''How can I? They didn't figure in the crime. One of the newspaper reporters—he looked up some of them at the time. A story said one was a dental hygienist. Another ran a flower shop. And by keeping my eyes open, I've got a line on a couple more. A brother lives in Bridgeport—no, I don't know where—and a sister has a house that's too hot at night in Peekskill, and another sister, Emmy Lou, the redhead, she lives in Paterson, New Jersey. Oh, yes. One of them reads a Newark paper. Phil, it's no use. All their addresses? No way unless we go to the parents.''

The desk lamp illumined the gloom embedded in his eyes. ''If we had their names and addresses, all of them pinpointed, I could arrange something. Would take some doing, but I could manage it. Eighteen men altogether, two on each family, the whole thing synchronized so nine doors would be pounded on at the same minute, no one having a chance to warn anyone else. Within let's say ten hours, I could have it set up. But if one of that crowd is in a position to spread the word . . .''

He was shaking his head, and she knew the vision he dispelled was the same as hers. An admonitory phone call. A child led out a back door into the night. A man panicking, resolved not to be caught. ''You mean, one of them might—''

''Lydia, don't say it.'' He went over to the window. When she used to walk with him down one of those blighted streets, she was always conscious of the peo-

ple watching them, lurking in doorways, behind
stoops, in parked cars, next to lampposts. In her mind,
an army waiting to spring, and at the same time de-
barred from it by his formidable presence.

Now the shapeless mound of his back was so still
she wondered what he had found of interest in the
configuration of roofs and towers outside. Or could
there be something dramatic going on in the street below? Then she understood. This is what time will be
like for her from now on. Any interval an exercise in
anguished waiting, every moment a blank sheet on
which imagination can write its worst. "Tell me again
what that man said. The brother-in-law," he finally
asked.

Her hoarse voice repeated it. "Good people underneath . . . wouldn't harm anyone."

"I think that's what they're counting on. That
you'll think they wouldn't harm her. But also, that
you'll do your part. Throw your weight around to
where they want it. So what's the story, Lydia? Would
you change the direction of the trial? Give them their
culprit? Would you let them have their wild justice?
Lydia, would you?"

The same question Diane had asked. This time she
was the one to be slow about answering. "Phil, remember what I was like in Legal Aid? Win, win, win.
My percentage of victories—well, you all knew it. But
what maybe you don't know, those victories didn't
come easy. Whether I thought my client was innocent
or guilty, I sacrificed everything to get him off. Plenty
of times I spent a weekend working on a summation.

I broke dates so I could dig up some obscure piece of law. Instead of going to the movies, I sat overtime in the library. I'm not complaining. It's what you do for clients who can't pay. What some of us do, anyhow. But this is different. Here the thing I'd sacrifice would be my own child. And I won't do it. No way. This time he's the one who gets sacrificed. This guy whose parents are paying plenty for his defense." The tears were starting again. Something about Phil's kindly protectiveness. "Besides, I never wholly trusted him. A nice guy, but there's something shady. A couple of times he hasn't come clean with me. About his car, his love life. Me, his lawyer—what's he hiding? I've never been able to figure it." She stopped walking up and down. "The answer to your question is yes. They can have their culprit. I'll hand him to them. His head on their platter."

He nodded. "So now you want to know what I'd do in your place. What I think I'd do. That's the terrible spot you have me in—right?" When he sighed, the sound seemed to come from deep in that bulky middle. "Okay. If it were me, I'd let it ride. Keep the police with their heavy-handed tactics out of it. I know. That lets you in for two days of the most godawful torment. I still think it's the prudent way. The way of most safety."

It was what she thought, she said quietly. She had just wanted to get it confirmed. After he left—after he hugged her and gave all the assurances about being available at any time day or night, and unhappily walked out—she sat in the desk chair he had vacated. Would she be willing to change the direction of the

trial? Both of them had asked it and got the same answer. So now her course was clear: first, to find that
discreditable aspect of Jerry Eldstrom that she claimed
was a part of everyone's life, and second, to decide
how best to introduce this new material at the trial.

But as she started through the notes she had made
during the interviews with Jerry, what she saw was not
the jagged line of her own private shorthand, but the
cold anger on Diane's face when she realized she was
being outmaneuvered. Lydia jabbed her pencil on the
desk top. A teacher like Diane feels good will and re-
spect for the women whose children she takes care of,
and concern and affection for the children themselves. But under all these benign emotions, there is
also—who doesn't sense it?—a substratum of what?
Envy? Bitterness? Resentment? It's mainly, of course,
because of the difference in pay. The women in their
classy business suits who make those breathless stops
every morning are rushing off, by and large, to high-
paying jobs, while the salary of nursery school teachers is lower than that of garbage collectors, policemen, department store clerks. And at times of stress,
this disparity can inflame the latent grievance. In the
aggrieved mind, "I understand why she has to leave
her child for ten hours a day" can modulate to "She
does, after all, walk out on her child for ten hours a
day" to emerge finally as "If she really loved her
child, she wouldn't leave her for ten hours a day."

It was surely a time of stress for Diane; at this very
moment, Lydia thought, she would be writhing under
just that kind of rancor. She would be sitting in her
room, her heavy features glowering as she brooded

about her injustice: an adored child put in jeopardy because of the intransigence of a negligent and undeserving mother. She, Lydia, had had second thoughts the moment she left the school; why else would she have called Phil? So what about Diane, whose first thoughts had never been anything to count on? "Do you promise to do it my way?" was the last thing Lydia had said. "I promise," Diane's sulky voice had answered. Sulky, resistant, unconvinced. Now she would think over that ill-gotten promise, and get up to stir some rosemary into her pork chops, and sit down to her solitary supper, and brood about it some more. The picture was vivid. Diane telling herself she takes care of the child, she's the one who knows what's best. Diane summoning all her powers of defiance and resolve. Diane walking with her awkward tread to the phone. Diane shrieking into it the irreversible alert.

Yes. That is exactly what will happen. Lydia stood and went to the phone herself. "Pat? Pat, it's Lydia."

"Since when do you have to tell me?"

Well, of course Pat Barlow would recognize her voice. Another single mother three floors above: one of the blessings of apartment-house living. When she was pregnant, she used to speculate about moving to the suburbs. "Imagine, Owen. A backyard, place for a swing, sidewalks for the kid to bike on." Wait till the kid is born," Owen would circumspectly answer— later, of course, she was to discover the real reason for his circumspection. But sometimes with a shiver she would think, Suppose Owen had given in and we had moved. Me alone now in some rambling, isolated house. Without that indispensable doorman, without a handyman to call if a window sticks, above all without Pat Barlow.

"Pat, listen. Is Janey around? Well, if she could do me the most terrific favor. I have these samples of wallpaper for Addie's room, and it's no use asking Addie, what does she know? I mean, how can she tell what she'll like three, four years from now? And what wallpaper costs these days, it better last four years. So if a six-year-old could cast her discerning eye... No, she isn't here. That's the whole point. Owen took her right from school. Yeah, big surprise, he actually remembered he was a father. Isn't it? July Fourth and all. Anyhow, now that the coast is clear, if Janey could come down for a sec. Yes, I saw the friend in the lobby, send them both."

They came—ah, elevators!—in two minutes. A couple of six-year-olds very solemn at being invested with such awesome responsibility. In here, she told them. If they would just hold up the papers one by one—like this—and sort of walk around and consider. They were darling to do this, she really thanked them. And while they're deciding, do they mind if she goes inside to make a quick phone call?

Their high-pitched voices, lavish with effusions about vines and red and white roses and pretty birds, reached her clearly. She, on the other hand, cupped her palm around her mouth to confine the words. "Diane? It's Lydia. Well, if I do, there's a reason. She's back. You heard me. Addie is back! You can hear her"—a quick shift of the mouthpiece to allow those bubbling cries to make their way across the wires. "Yes. With Janey Barlow. This child who lives upstairs. Oh, Diane, I don't know. Ten minutes ago, there was just a call from the doorman. Miss Ness, your little girl is down here. So I flew down, and there she was. No. Just that a car left her off. He did give me a funny look. I guess he thinks I have some irresponsible friends, to leave a three-year-old off on her own. But I didn't want to ask too many questions, and I surely don't want to press Addie—Diane, don't you agree? Well, just that some people drove her, and they gave her a sandwich and ice cream, and brought her home. And since she's all right, she seems to be all right"—another tilt of the phone toward that other room: solemnity had turned to plainly audible giggles. "Must be that. Those people. But instead of keeping her till the trial, like we thought, there was just this warning. Oh, believe me. She won't be out of my sight tomorrow. And Diane, I may not bring her in on Thursday either, you'll understand. Yes, I know you are. Me too. Oh, God, me too."

She hung up. She's done it. Diane mollified. Diane unable to take action—she's carried it off. But then why can't she move? Why is it such a burden to rise and take the half-dozen steps to the next room and keep herself upright at the door? Why is she so choked with fury at the sight of children doing what children always do, which is to play with whatever toys are at hand? They had taken Addie's circus set off the shelf—the miniature clown, the woman in a blue tutu, the spangled horse—and set it on the rug. She drew in her breath. How dare they! Such nerve! Such presumption! Alien fingers touching Addie's things, handling the small wooden figures for which Addie has her own routine, her own special arrangement.

"That's enough now, children," she said.

They stared at her as they eased out: two girls wearing shorts, sleeveless shirts, puzzled expressions. It wasn't till she heard the elevator that she realized: she didn't ask them about the wallpaper that was the alleged reason for their visit.

Well, now she knows. She has to watch it. She can put on an act, all right, but she has to watch it. The truth is, had one of those children lingered, stayed to play longer with that circus set, she, Lydia Ness, would have slapped her. Her hand tingled, as if it had come in contact with that smooth rosy cheek that offended by not being Addie's.

She went back to her desk. Keep working, that's what's going to save her sanity. Going over every word spoken by Jerry until she finds that crucial area of vulnerability. But how can you work when the phone rings? At first she thought of not answering. She let it ring twice. Then she raced over. Suppose it's them. Calling with an ultimatum, an apology, a warning, a promise about Addie.

"Hello? Oh, Owen, you."

"Who'd you think it was going to be?"

She gathered her strength. "Owen, how's everything?"

"Lydia, you sure you're all right? At first you sounded so— Well, everything is not so hot, now that you ask."

"Owen, look. Right now I—"

"It's Uncle Leo," he said. "Marcy's Uncle Leo. Didn't I tell you about him? He's not a bad sort, not as objectionable as Uncle Charlie, for instance. But his wife just left him. After twenty-two years, Brenda walks off with this fellow eight years younger than she is. So my heart goes out to Uncle Leo, naturally it does. And he was nice to Marcy when she was twelve or thirteen, I'm not exactly clear, but some special dispensation. So when she asks him to stay for a weekend, I can understand. Even, let's say, four days. But when two weeks go by... Two weeks and no sign of leaving. He shows travelogues, Lyd. Never mind that Brenda is the main character. He wants us to look at his travelogues."

Any other time she would have laughed. Laughed and advised a course of action that combined resourcefulness with accommodation. Poor Owen, who had inherited uncles, cousins, nephews, grandmothers, and unappealing school chums along with that cute Marcy.

She shuffled her papers. "Owen, I'm sorry."

"...going to this club where everyone reports on travels so long as it's exotic, Marcy is taking him. So that leaves me free for her."

"Her?"

"Lyddy, aren't you listening? Addie. I told you. What a day I've planned. Crack of dawn to this friend on Long Island who has his own beach, she'll have a ball, and then lunch, and she can nap, I guess, in the car, and then supper for the two of us at that place she really—"

"No."

"Lyddy, it's not what you think. This friend has his own child. A year younger than Addie, but—"

"I said no."

"What's that?" Owen clutched his hair when a conversation in some way went against him. His hand would be up now, grabbing the graying, curly strands.

"Addie can't go."

"I don't get it."

"We made plans. Douglas and I. We're taking her for the whole day."

"This way you and Douglas can be free. A bonanza. You can go to a museum. Tea dancing. Watch firecrackers."

"We want to be with Addie." Amazing: her normal voice got that out.

"Lyddy, you're not really telling me that stuffed shirt Douglas would rather— Okay. Skip that. Skip it." He sounded penitential. There was in truth no malice in Owen. Ingenuousness, naiveté, muddled thinking, weakness, but no malice. "What I mean is, a child in the city so much, she could use a day on a beach, she definitely needs it."

"That's really cute, Owen. You ignore her for months on end, that time she had the flu we didn't hear from you for six weeks, and then you're ready to prescribe where she ought to play."

"I thought we agreed that I'd have holidays and every other weekend."

"We also agreed that if you wanted her you'd let me know two days in advance. Here it is eight at night—" She looked at the clock. Eight-fifteen. Addie has been gone for two hours and fifteen minutes.

Silence at the other end. Fair-minded as always, Owen would be turning this over, concurring with the basic concept, searching for an acceptable loophole. He grabbed a handful of hair—she could see it—before he spoke again.

"Lyddy, let me talk to her. We'll make plans for some other time."

"She's not here. No, I am not just saying that to punish you, she isn't here. Owen, I swear to you Addie is not here. She's up at the Barlows'. Yes, I know it's late, but I have a lot of work, in case you didn't—"

"Hey, don't think I'm not proud. There was a story on TV just an hour ago. A picture of you, well, an artist's picture, and that Eldstrom fellow, and one of the girl's family. They said from the looks of it Eldstrom would probably be acquitted. Lyddy, you really did it, didn't you?"

"That's right," she said. "I did it."

"I can tell. You want me to hang up."

"Owen, it's nothing personal. But I—"

"I won't keep you. But you tell Addie her old man has a gold necklace for her with this little blue heart on it. Will you do that?"

When she hung up, she saw her blouse was wet. She washed, and changed her clothes, and made a sandwich that she was unable to get down, and she was starting to work again when the doorbell rang. Dear God, help me. Let it be them.

"Lydia, you can't fool me. Something's going on. Am I right?"

"Hello, Pat."

Pat slid past her, a tall, dark, thin woman who could manage to look elegant even in the shorts and shirt into which she'd changed when she came home from her job as a bank vice president. Now she sat on the arm of a chair. "I wouldn't have come just on the children's say so. Even though they did have a sort of garbled report. Something about your wanting their judgment and also not wanting it. But when Owen gets in the act, too."

"Owen?"

"Lydia, your ex-husband, remember? Same relation to you as Ernesto is to me." Pat liked to perch on the arms of chairs. It gave her an air of impermanence, of transience, that was wholly at odds with the careful attention she invariably gave to a conversation. Now she wiped her brow. "Lydia, my God. Ninety-two outside—since when are you against air-conditioning?"

"Sorry. I forgot to turn it on." She followed Pat's gaze around the living room. Once when she decided to buy curtains for the two windows, she ordered one fabric, and then canceled it to choose another with a slightly different weave, and then canceled both to wait six months for still another. Was that possible? Did she once possess the equanimity to devote that kind of absorbed deliberation to the selection of cream-colored gauze for a window?

"What's Owen got to do with anything?"

"He just called. He seemed to be under the impression that Addie was at our house, and he wanted to talk to her. Something, I gathered, about a gold necklace." Her gaze, concerned and censorious at once, looked around. "Where the hell is Addie, if you don't mind my asking?"

The impulse to tell was suddenly insuperable. To have an ally, a support, a confidante.

But of course she would not have an ally. She would have an opponent, an adversary, just as Diane had been. She looked at that taut, nervy figure and she knew exactly what Pat would say. It's your decision, Lydia, but if it were my child, I can tell you what I'd do. I'd have every police and detective and FBI man in the country alerted. I'd use every bit of influence anyone I knew possessed to make them put on the heat. I'd have those people's houses surrounded—where'd you say they live? New Jersey? Connecticut? Three right here in New York? Believe me, Lydia, an army would besiege every one.

Hearing those didactic certitudes, it all would start again. Her own doubts. The doubts that in truth never left her. The concept of an army, after all, is an appealing one. The vigor, the martial authority, the manly force. She would explain to Pat about the nature of those people, and she also would cite the hazards that are possible for a child when the kidnapper feels cornered, but even as she methodically laid the arguments out, she would sense herself weakening. Pat's sharp gaze would turn compellingly toward her. That delusively easy path counseled by Diane, by Pat, would look comforting, inviting.

Where is Addie? Pat was waiting.

"You'll laugh at me when I tell you this."

"Trust me."

"I have a date with Douglas."

"What's new about that? Wasn't that Douglas I saw you with last Tuesday, when I was going to—"

"A special date. We decided—oh, Lord, I sound like a blooming adolescent—we decided to see what it would be like to be together for a whole night."

"Lydia, stop me if I'm stepping over the line, but I always took for granted you and Doug—"

"Oh, sure, I sleep with him. But always on the run. That is, in his apartment, with the attendant nuisance of my having to get up and get dressed and come home. So we thought we'd see what an uninterrupted night would be like."

"Lydia, is this a preliminary to maybe a bigger relationship?"

"Maybe." She put out her hands.

Pat crossed the room, she went to the arm of the couch. "More nosiness on my part, but I always had the impression you thought Douglas was something of a...a..."

"A prig. Right. But a prig might be what I need in my life right now. Someone utterly staid and rigid and responsible. Anyhow"—for God's sake, she has to speed this up—"you can see why I didn't want to say all this to Owen."

Pat nodded. She could certainly see.

"So I just said Addie was at your house, when the thing is, she's spending the night at one of the teachers'. From nursery school, I mean. The woman will take wonderful care. She has children of her own. Girls, eight and ten. Addie's met them, she'll have fun with them. I mean, even though it's a big thing for her, away from home for a whole night, she'll be with people who love her and—"

"Hey, Lyddy, you can skip the details. Naturally I know if you actually let Addie go some place overnight, it's where she's going to be safe and feel comfortable."

When she jolted her arm, a pile of magazines fell to the floor.

"As if I haven't heard the way you carry on about a sitter who's going to stay for just three hours." Pat swung her bare, bony leg along the side of the couch. "Addie can't be left with her until you get her whole life history, and references from four people, and for all I know her voting record for the past two—"

"Pat, I really should get, um, ready."

"Oh, honey, I hope it's great. With Douglas, that is. Wonderful woman like you, you really do deserve—"

What does she deserve? The question she has been asking herself all evening. Surely not the person who now rang the doorbell. Because when she went to answer it, Douglas stood there.

TWELVE

"OWEN CALLED ME with some misinformation about tomorrow." To the point, as always, Douglas greeted her at the door.

"Shh. Tell me later. Pat Barlow's here," she explained.

They knew each other, she superfluously said when she led Douglas into the living room. In truth, they knew each other better than either one suspected. Doug knew about the succession of women with whom Pat's ex-husband Ernesto had entertained himself, culminating in the one he had invited to stay for three weeks in their apartment. As for Pat, on the weekend afternoons when their respective children were playing on some jungle gym or watching the polar bear at the zoo or dripping ice cream cones on their best dresses, she had participated in countless discussions about why Lydia was disinclined to marry Doug. His rigidity, his iron composure, his structured life.

Pat wasn't thinking about structure and composure now; that was evident from her shining eyes, the heightened swing of her bony ankle as she sat on the arm of the couch. She was delighted to see him, she said. He probably wanted to congratulate Lydia for the job she was doing at the trial. Such arguments! Such brilliance! Such intimations of success!

She had appropriated their evening, Lydia saw, cherishing what was novel about it, exaggerating what was illicit, deluding herself about what was momentous. When she started an animated conversation with Douglas now, it was not to delay that alleged tryst, but rather to encourage it, help bring it to fruition.

The conversation was about Pat's bank. Or, rather, the building that housed it. The lobby had just been redone with much glass, a riotous collection of plants, and a large and overwrought mural, a development Pat approved and Douglas predictably deplored.

"But Douglas, I don't see why you object so strenuously," Pat said. "Handsome artwork to greet people as they come in. It gives a building grace and elegance."

"Banking isn't meant to be graceful and elegant. It should be sound and trustworthy."

"Doug, come on. You mean, you'd really excommunicate all ornament? Just have some big blank front?" Pat looked ornamental herself, her gaze quizzical, her long legs swinging.

"I think customers should come in because of what they know of a bank's reputation, not because some trivial embellishment in the lobby attracts them."

"Goodness. I'd think you'd be just the one in favor of freer forms. I mean, engineering today—it makes so many solutions possible."

"I'm in favor of a building that expresses functional effectiveness," Douglas said stiffly.

They would be good for each other, Lydia thought; both obviously enjoyed batting these argumentative balls back and forth. It was their sole form of aggressiveness. Their voices might take on a strident, even a truculent, pitch in debate, but in actuality both were good-hearted, generous, caring. Yes, Pat and Doug. Definitely a match. Maybe when all this was over she would work on it. Pat wouldn't mind Doug's sobriety, his soldierly air of officialdom; she might even welcome it after the years of Ernesto's capricious and sadistic unfaithfulness. And Doug would admire just that soundness and responsibility Pat indubitably put into the guardianship of other people's money.

But not now. Now she has to get them both out of here fast. She gave Pat a meaningful look which that shrewed woman interpreted correctly. She had to run, Pat said. Those two children she's left upstairs, Lord knows what they will be up to. Their third TV program, probably, though they know that one is the absolute limit. She kissed Lydia, an unusual gesture denoting complicity and approval.

Well, it's an unusual evening. Lydia sat back, while Douglas, speaking with his practiced punctilio, explained again why he was here. Owen had called him, he said. "Such an odd conversation. I know Owen was excited, but still I'm fairly sure I heard correctly. What he said was he understood I was going to spend the day with you and Addie tomorrow. The whole day. And he knew how I must be looking forward to it, but he wondered if he could induce me to change. Because it was really important to him to have Addie. Something about a beach. A beach and friends and sun and sand. And he'd made no headway with you, so he was taking a chance and trying me."

"I see."

His honest eyes regarded her. "Lydia, this is the first time I hear that you and I have a date for tomorrow, much less a date with your child."

"Doug, do you want a drink?"

His hand brushed this aside. The fact is, he would have asked Lydia to spend time with him tomorrow. A midweek holiday—obvious. But he took for granted she'd be too busy because of the trial to consider any interruption. But now an interruption had been, so to speak, proposed, he wanted Lydia to know he was perfectly willing to spend the day with her and Addie. Not just willing, delighted. But he did have some problems about what the program should be. He had listened to the weather report. Between ninety and ninety-five predicted for tomorrow. Well. A sweltering day in the city with a small child. If it were a weekend, of course there would be no question. They could drive to some nice resort, give them all a healthy time in the sun. But to get into the hassle of traffic for a single day—he didn't think Lydia would welcome that. Especially since he knew what a strain she must be under. So he had been turning over in his mind possible activities. One of those horse-driven carriages in the park, Addie might like that. The ride took, he understood, one hour.

The droning voice paused. She could see the computation going on inside that sincere head. Start ride at ten, get back at eleven. Still nine hours of daylight to account for.

Or a children's movie, he went on. Some, he had heard, were quite charming. He remembered one himself. About a deer, was it? He didn't know if it was appropriate for a three-year-old, Lydia would of course be the expert on that. The zoo he believed they must dismiss. On July Fourth, too crowded. But perhaps there was some program at a museum? He believed there were pamphlets that dealt with just such contingencies, but unfortunately he had not had time to equip himself before he came.

She knew she should stop him. She wanted desperately to stop him, but if she did they would move inevitably to the next phase, which was why she had lied to Owen. Well, why did she lie to Owen? At the moment, she had no idea. She couldn't think. She felt depleted, an empty vessel. You could crank and crank, and not another inventive story would come out.

He was still going on. A playground? A restaurant adapted for children? Some program—could there be one?—designed around a patriotic theme? Fireworks of course in the evening, but he doubted whether this was suitable, what did Lydia think?

What she thought was that he was the one—the only one—who would agree with her course of action. He would scrutinize the facts and weigh the options, and in the end he would definitely agree. Emotion wouldn't enter into his clear-headed assessment. He wouldn't see a child with bangs cut straight across, dazzling eyes, as Diane did, as Pat would. He would see a case history: X is kidnapped—how to get X back in the most efficacious way. He would apply his methodical mind to this problem as he did to the problem of how to entertain a small child on a hot July day, and he would come up with the obvious answer: you do what the kidnappers want. Yes, he would say, the disadvantages inherent in any other course are plain. If you alerted these people, let them think they were cornered, there is definitely the chance that they would—She put her hands over her ears, as if to exclude the words. Doug spelling out the hazards, citing other cases of kidnappers who had been led by panic and fear of disclosure into doing unintended harm.

She has no desire to confide in him, and yet she knows that of all of them, Douglas is the one who would support her.

"... so that's what I wonder," he said.

"What?"

"Lydia, are you listening? I said, I wonder why you told Owen such an unlikely story." And when she didn't immediately answer, he added that he must apologize for dropping in. As she knows, it is not something he generally does. But he had been on the way out, and he was so disturbed by the call, he thought it best to share the disturbance with her. Because if it means there is trouble—well, she knows he's ready at all times to be of service.

She looked out the window. She lived on the fifteenth floor; past the fastidiously selected curtains, the view spoke of distance, of isolation, of nebulous and inhospitable vistas. Out there somewhere, a child was incommunicado. "No trouble," she said.

He paused. He didn't want to probe, he said with awkward delicacy. Certainly not. They've always understood that she's free to go anyplace, see anyone. As he would be, if he so desired.

His delicacy was what she needed. Of course. Obvious. He has given her the cue. "Doug, I didn't want to hurt you."

"So I'm right." The martial shoulders straightened.

She looked down. There was a glass ashtray on the table, and she twirled it.

"What's he like. The new man?"

"That's it. I hardly know myself. I simply wanted a chance to get better acquainted." She moved to the other side of the room, where the lamp didn't cast its insistent glow. "But also I didn't want to give Owen wrong ideas. You know how he is. He's made me his confidante, his counselor. God, the problems he expects me to deal with. Sometimes I think I know more about his marriage than Marcy does." She stopped. In the hall the elevator door was opening. Nothing. No one. Someone from the other apartment. "But because he's taken me willy-nilly into his life, he thinks it should be a two-way street. He's entitled to be proprietary about me. He can seize on anything I do and make it his business. I mean, it's all a little crazy. He chose to get out of my life, but in his mixed-up way he still wants to be in it. So I thought this once I'd by-pass him. I realize it was a dumb thing to do. Using your name. If I'd had any idea he was going to drag you in..."

She came back to her first seat. In some philosophy course at college, the professor had given a lecture on lying. Lydia suddenly remembered that high-pitched voice—it was a woman—and she could see her own scribbled handwriting as she struggled to keep up with

the portentous words. "Lying; undesirable conse-
quences of. 1. A liar diminishes himself, his integrity,
his dignity. 2. After the first lie, the others come more
easily, irresistibly, as moral distinctions coarsen and
more deceit is needed to bolster the original story. 3.
The harm that lying does is cumulative and hard to
reverse."

Well, all that is true, God knows tonight she's
proved it. But what it neglected to say, that remon-
strative voice, was that when you lie you simply talk
too much. You elaborate. You go in for an unaccustomed and unattractive garrulity. You concentrate so
assiduously on the small portion of your talk that is
the truth that you dredge up gratuitous and possibly
damaging details.

What she'd said about Owen happened to be correct. But not only was it unnecessary, it pained Douglas to hear it, it clouded what was an already a murky
situation.

"Lydia, do you mind if I ask you something?"

"Feel free."

"This whole"—he cleared his throat—"misunder-
standing. Is it really about Addie?"

"What do you mean?"

"I know how she comes first with you. Her welfare
above everything. Oh, Lydia dear, don't deny it. How
it should be. So I was wondering. This other man—is
it because you consider him more, um, suitable for
Addie than I am?"

"Oh, Doug, nothing like it." A miracle: she can
turn on him her look of propitiating equanimity.

"I know I'm stiff with her. I have no experience—I've told you this—playing with a child. Even in my own family. Just me and that much older brother." He took a pen out of his pocket and put it back. "But because I'm not demonstrative, sometimes I hang back, that doesn't mean . . . Well, I was talking about Addie to someone in my office the other day. One of those conversations that happen to turn on children. So this fellow described his child, and then I heard myself going on about Addie. So adorable, is what I said. All bounce and brains and cuteness. And I realized how true it is. What she means to me. So even though I may not make the right noises about a doll—Lydia, you all right?"

She bent over the table. "Yes. Sure."

"I didn't mean to push it. I know you're uncomfortable when I push it."

At any other time, she would have been touched. His self-criticism could not have come easy. He was one of those men whose stance says, Here I am, this is it, take it or leave it. He didn't scrutinize his buildings once they were completed, he knew what went into them was of sterling quality—no more did he find it necessary to scrutinize himself. But here he was, this bluff soldier, explaining how he really felt more affection than he was able to show.

Maybe, after all, I should have told him the truth, she thought. But she thought it too late. By then, the elevator had long since taken him down, and she was reading for the third time the notes on her first interview with Jerry Eldstrom.

THIRTEEN

ONCE WHEN SHE WAS in the hospital with what had been misdiagnosed as a thyroid problem, she heard the woman in the next bed talking to the nurse. "I can't go through the night with this pain," the woman said in her calm, matter-of-fact voice. "They've told me all the reasons why more medication is contraindicated, but I simply cannot bear it. That's how it is. I'll die first—you can tell the doctor. I cannot endure eight hours with this suffering."

Well, in the morning the woman was still behind the folds of flowered curtain, and by midafternoon she was taking a few steps accompanied by the nurse and the spindly IV pole, and at suppertime she sat in a chair while the tray of soft foods was put before her.

Lydia thought of it now. That voice with its assured, mistaken declaration. The fact is, you can get through a night of intolerable suffering. You are sure you won't, but you do. You endure. You somehow do the impossible, which is to survive the eight o'clock hour that marks a child's bathtime and the eight-thirty one when you read her one story and then on urgent request another and then—Please, Mommy—still another, and the nine o'clock turning point when, all the stuffed animals having been ritualistically arranged, lights are definitely out, and the bleary time around two when the patter of rain or the blare of a distant

siren wakes you and for no reason except your own
peace of mind you go to check on the small bed—you
get through it all, and in the morning, feeling battered, groggy, you go about your business.

Her business this morning was to see Brian Ahearn,
who was the principal of Pendil Park High School,
and for an uneasy interval, it seemed as if the business of Mrs. Ahearn was to keep this meeting from
taking place.

"You mothers. Badger him day in and out." She
was a short, plump woman whose sweet features gave
every indication of generally being arranged in a less
aggrieved expression. Now she stood on the porch of
their comfortable shingled house as if prepared to
physically bar the way. "Seven days a week," that
stormy voice went on. "Fifty-two weeks a year. Including summer. It's not fair. That poor, put-upon
man. What did he have—three days between regular
school and summer school? So what is it this time?
Your child's science teacher doesn't understand him?
He needs a special letter from the principal to make it
into college? Or is it maybe an excuse to come ten
minutes late every morning because of his tennis les-
sons? Well, I won't have it. A holiday. His one day.
And in his own house, too—I will not let him be disturbed. Besides"—a cagy shift in tactics—"he's not
even home. He went down to the village to get a
newspaper."

A series of thumps from a space under the porch
cast some doubt on this assertion. Mrs. Ahearn
stepped back valiantly toward the door. Then she

frowned. "You don't look old enough to be the mother of a high school kid."

"I'm not."

"Well, why didn't you—"

"I'm Lydia Ness. I'm representing Jerry Eldstrom."

The woman stared. "You're right. It really is you. Representing that poor boy—good gracious, I should have recognized. You're better looking than that artist makes out. Well, come in, then." She led Lydia onto the straw rug of the hall, then she opened the door to the cellar. "Brian? Brian dear? Someone to see you about—" The hammering continued. "He does carpentry," she explained. "It's his one relaxation. But once he gets started, you can't—Brian!"

More hammering.

"I'll go down," the woman unwillingly said, gazing at the steep steps.

"Let me. It's all right. If he just knew I was coming."

This time he heard. "A young lady? Send her down."

He was at his worktable when she went. He was as short as his wife, and stouter, and he greeted her with the practiced affability of one used to producing a greeting on short notice at all hours for perfect strangers. What could he do for her?

His face lit up when she told him. "Something about Jerry Eldstrom? Shall I let you in on a tiny secret? I was wondering why you didn't ask. His high school principal, after all. Don't they always ask?"

She nodded. That was the portion of her notes she had played over and over: There's Mr. Ahearn, my high school principal, I'm sure he'd have a good word— No, on second thought don't call him, Jerry had said. And with nothing at stake, she had listened.

Mr. Ahearn put down his hammer. He said from reading the newspaper accounts it was his impression the trial was almost over.

"Things can change," she said. "Even at the last minute things can change."

"So you might want me to testify? About the boy's good character?" His eyes showed his eagerness. POPULAR HIGH SCHOOL PRINCIPAL TESTIFIES IN RAPE TRIAL.

She looked around the cellar. The light from four fluorescent bulbs shone on tools, wood, blueprints, piles of sawdust. She wanted him to tell her anything he could remember about Jerry, she said.

"I did look him up when I read about it. One of our boys accused of that terrible crime, of course I got out all his records. But remember him? Me personally? I wish I could say yes." He paused, but only to listen to the footsteps overhead. Mrs. Ahearn going to the door again, turning off someone else who wanted to bother her husband on his holiday? "We have eighteen hundred students, Miss Ness. You remember the ones at either end. The very bright ones, who sail through the AP courses and get written up as whiz kids and walk off with the prizes at graduation. And also the troublemakers, whose teachers beg you to expel them once and for all because how can they teach social studies with that disruption in the back row. But that great mass in the middle—the ones who aren't caught selling dope in the boys' room or cheating on a test or impregnating a girl behind the auditorium—I regret to say they go unnoticed.''

He shook his head; despite the short stature, an air of authority would emanate from him when he cared to use it, Lydia thought. ''Well, Jerry Eldstrom—actually I have his papers here at home. Mrs. A. and I were talking about him, and she was curious to know what he was like. So we'll go up in a minute. But first I have to put the clamps on this piece, do you mind?''

She gave the only possible answer.

''It's a shelf to go above Mrs. A.'s dressing table, so I want it to have a beautiful surface. That's why I'm using veneer. And these new resin glues, they don't dry too fast, there's time for even an amateur like me to get the veneer on exactly straight.''

Even from where she was standing, she could see it was not going to be exactly straight. At one corner, the veneer had edged away from the underlying wood by a fraction of an inch.

He may have followed her gaze. ''The truth is, I'm not very good. Mr. Pintard, he's the shop teacher at school, he wouldn't put up with me for a second. He insists on perfection. Considering the competition the boys will have to meet when they get out, he's right to insist on perfection. I don't let it bother me. I like working down here; it gets me away from my problems. And Mrs. A. is nice about it. She pretends she likes what I make. Well, Miss Ness, shall we go up?''

They went through a living room where a bookcase with rough edges and a coffee table with sides that were not precisely even attested to Mrs. Ahearn's tolerance, and into a small study beyond. The desk in here also looked homemade: Mr. Ahearn had to perform some intricate manipulations on the drawer, jiggling it first one way and then the other, before it would open.

"Now. Where were we? Yes. Jerry Eldstrom. I have everything here. What do you want to know?"

I want to know why he first proposed my talking to you and then rescinded it. I want to know that you have been concealing the fact that he once raped a girl and stuffed her body in the utility closet. It's necessary that I find out something startling about him that will change the course of the trial.

"Should we start with his marks?" he said. "Straight C plus average. I've never been able to discern a difference between B minus and C plus. The latter, I suspect, means simply that the teacher is tired, disgruntled, disaffected, and perhaps has had a fight with his or her fiancée the previous evening. In any case, none of them were willing to grant him that extra bonus. C plus it is." Mr. Ahearn looked down at the transcript. "He failed physics his junior year but took it again in summer school and squeaked by with an ignoble but passing D. And once he pulled down an A minus in intermediate algebra—I suppose he came up with a couple of bright answers in class and the teacher was momentarily fooled. Anyhow, by midyear he was down to B, and he finished—look, you can see—with that swinging C."

She averted her eyes from the photocopied columns. "There must be something else. Besides marks, I mean."

"Let's look at what they say about him in the yearbook. Jerry Eldstrom: 'Directs traffic for Parking Lot Committee . . . has friendly smile for everyone . . . dislikes study halls . . . captain of bowling team in sophomore year.' Nothing much to single him out—You look disappointed, Miss Ness. Suppose we compare him with the fellow under him. Mark Ellis. 'Guided misled students as a Traffic Squad member . . . tinkers with cars in spare time . . . flips for girls . . . often seen bending over a cue stick.' See what I mean? You can't tell one from the other. One bowls and one shoots pool, but that's about it. 'Bending over a cue stick,'" Mr. Ahearn repeated sadly. "That record of undifferentiated mediocrity, I don't know why they're so avid to have it inscribed in glossy black and white for posterity. Once someone suggested—I forgot who the genius was—that the yearbook be omitted. Just one year, don't have it. All the effort, after all, that goes into that inglorious compilation: the makeup, the advertising, the pictures, the production. And then, senior year, each of them having to shell out more than most of them can readily afford. But they want it. It appears in their young fatuousness they really do want it. Sometimes I think they're more conservative, our high school students, even than their parents. Anyhow, an uproar went up about the suggestion to end it. Deprive themselves of their precious yearbook? Never."

He closed the book with its shiny red cover and sighed. "Don't get me wrong, Miss Ness. They're nice kids, most of them. Undifferentiated, did I say? That's my fault. I'm the one who doesn't have time to differentiate them. When I started at Pendil Park—I won't say how many years ago that was—I taught a course myself. American history. Keeping my hand in. Every day at eleven I could stand in front of thirty eager faces and talk about the Constitutional Convention. Heaven. These days—I don't have to tell you the problems when you're handling teenagers. Do you have a child, Miss Ness?"

"She's three."

"Ah, then you don't know what trouble is." He rubbed his hand along the surface of his desk. "Sex, drugs, crime, you name it—I'm lucky, sitting at my desk every minute, if I can get through the day. It even follows me home—no aspersions, Miss Ness. I don't even have time to read my own books. Pick one up from that shelf over there—go on, any one at random. That's what I mean. That dust. Incidentally, did my wife give you a hard time? She means well. She just wants to protect me. If it were up to her, I wouldn't even be in the phone book. A public servant, I tell her—I owe it to them. It's my life."

The pleasant voice shaded into wistfulness. Maybe years ago he'd envisioned his life differently. Not presiding over that sea of mediocrity but turning out some inspired tome on history. A new revealing angle on the Constitutional Convention. She thumbed through the yearbook. "So there's nothing else?"

"Doesn't seem to be."

"Then why wouldn't he want you to testify?"

Mr. Ahearn looked up. "Jerry didn't want me?"

"That's why I didn't come before. He first mentioned you when I was asking him for character witnesses, and then said skip it."

He shook his head. "I can't imagine. If it were anything discreditable that I might know about, it would be here in the files of his guidance counselor. But look. A blank. He never even bothered to go to his guidance counselor, the boy with the friendly smile for everyone. There's just a note that he was thinking of going to electronics school, which I assume didn't pan out." He was watching her. "Don't fret, Miss Ness. I'm still glad to testify if you need me. He must have been a nice fellow and I'm delighted to say so."

"Thanks." It can't end like this. Hope turned off in the small, dusty study of a house in Pendil Park. Someone was setting off premature firecrackers outside—"Strictly illegal," Ahearn murmured—and she looked out the window. Willis, recruited to work on the holiday, was standing beside the car. They had one more stop, but what was the use, if it was going to be like this? Should she phone the police from here? Head fast to the nearest police station? Enlist Ben to call them? Yes, Ben with his manifold connections, his vast influence, that would be best.

But not enough influence to save a child if someone holding her started to panic.

"You look tired, Miss Ness. My wife makes a delicious lemonade, perfect for a hot day. Or something stronger? Gin and tonic?" The public servant, still putting on his dutiful courtesy.

"No, thanks."

"The papers say they expect acquittal. They're usually right, those reporters. So you have nothing to worry about, do you?"

"No. Nothing to worry about." She looked down at the photocopied pages while Ahearn struggled again with the recalcitrant drawer; "Awful the way wood sticks in all this dampness," he was mumbling.

"This word here. At the bottom of his transcript," she said. "What does it mean?"

He gave the drawer a final useless tug. "Hmm. Menotti, it looks like. Goodness, it comes back to me now. I suppose the guidance counselor made a note after all."

"Something about Jerry Eldstrom?"

"Don't get your expectations up, Miss Ness. He didn't win a math contest or get elected to student council or lead the band at half time. But there was something rather sweet. I don't know how I forgot it."

"Ah." She nodded listlessly. Sweetness—what in this instance she has no use for.

"I wasn't the one it happened to—I guess it's why it slipped my mind. It was John Menotti, one of the biology teachers. He told me—now I see it all—that Jerry one day bumped into his car in the parking lot. Nothing serious, just some paint scraped off. He knew it was Jerry because he got a quick look at the license and then checked with the office where we have license numbers of all the students' cars on file. Basic precaution. Making sure no car that's not registered uses the lot." His hand stroked the book she had pulled out: a love tap. "Anyhow, next day Mr.

Menotti called Jerry down and told him the damage
was six hundred dollars worth, and if Jerry couldn't
pay, he could work every afternoon for a month helping clean up the biology lab. The boy was very nice
about it, Menotti said. No complaints. No whining.
Sure, sure, he'd do the work. So the four weeks were
coming to an end when another student came in to say
Mr. Menotti had the wrong guy. It wasn't Jerry at all.
It was his brother.'' Mr. Ahearn got the drawer closed
at last. "That's high school for you. Wait long enough
and the truth eventually comes out. I see it every
time.''

"Jerry never told me he had a brother.''

"A brother, all right. Elliott—I remember now. One
year younger.''

"Why would he not mention it?''

"Lots of times they don't. They're good to the kid,
watch over him, take the gaff for him—well, look at
Jerry cleaning that lab all month long—but some
innate pride or misconceived guilt interferes, and they
don't bring it up in public.''

"Something wrong with this Elliott?''

"Well, 'wrong,' Miss Ness. I'm their principal. It's
my place to accept all kinds. Competent or not.''

"Elliott is retarded?''

"We try not to use the word. Anyhow,'' he went on,
"if you were looking for a way to make Jerry look
good, here you have it. Because a jury must admit it's
a kindly thing for a boy to do. Try to cover up for his
brother. Misguided but basically kindly.''

"If this Elliott isn't, um, competent, how come he
was driving?''

"That's the whole point. Somehow he got hold of Jerry's keys and took off with his car."

"How incompetent is he?"

"Oh, Miss Ness, there's no clear line. I remember at the time I looked Elliott up in the files, and he had an IQ in the low sixties. That put him in our special education class. Those classes—I wish they were as effective as they are special. In theory, students with learning problems get taken care of. In practice, we bow to the budget and lump them all together. The ones with low IQ's, and those with severe physical defects like multiple sclerosis, and even some with gross behavior problems like being hyperactive, and the resulting stew isn't exactly right for anyone."

"What happened to Elliott?"

"You mean, did he ever swipe his brother's car or bump into John Menotti again?" Mr. Ahearn gave a regretful wave, as if invoking that mass of eighteen hundred students. If he could only keep track of how they all turned out, he said.

"Could I speak to Mr. Menotti?"

"He's on sabbatical, lucky man. Six months in Europe. A privilege that's not afforded to principals. And now, Miss Ness . . ." He gave a meaningful tug at the drawer: time to move on. She roused herself.

"Oh, sure." She thanked him. She thanked him profusely. She told him to thank his wife. She said again no thank you to lemonade. Then she went out to the car.

"Willis, you know that second address I gave you? That's where we're going now."

FOURTEEN

SHE WAITED FOR HIM in the garden—what the attendant called a garden. It was a gently inclined sweep of lawn directly under the long porch of a long, low building. Behind her was a bed of annuals that obviously received daily care, and ahead, at the end of the lawn, a fringe of pine trees led into a shaded area. She kept standing, though there were plenty of places where she might sit: little clusters of white wrought-iron chairs placed around similarly painted tables. She had made her way up the hierarchy to get this far; people, it appeared, did not call unannounced on residents of Rockhaven Retirement Home. Mr. Chubb did not expect her? He didn't even know her? And yet she thought he would consent to see her? These unsavory facts were repeated over and over as she was passed from an attendant on the porch to a maid in blue uniform, to a nurse, to someone called the Director of Hospitality, to the director herself. But once connections were made, permission was given. A vulgar air of excitement even accompanied the final edict, that Stanley was to take Miss Ness into the garden, where Mr. Chubb would come soon.

Come how? In a wheelchair? With the aid of a walker? A cane? After four hours at the telephone, Tony had ascertained the name of the home where Mr. Chubb was a resident, but not the nature of the infirmity that had put him there. Would he have a blanket over his legs, like the two women being wheeled to the opposite side of the grass? As soon as his escort left, would he call in a parched voice to be moved elsewhere? Would he insistently demand a drink? She had been glad not to go into the building itself. It was an impressive, even a handsome structure, with fresh yellow paint on its facade and rambling wings on either side, but she had no wish to encounter the muffled smells, the tawdry air of cheeriness, the grimly utilitarian furniture she envisioned inside. But as more and more people strolled down to the chairs, she thought even one of those terrible rooms would be better if they could just have some privacy.

In fact, they had ample privacy. Stanley appeared again to say she should come along, Mr. Chubb was ready now. He led her along a path to a wisteria-shaded arbor where a gray-haired man wearing a navy jacket with nautical buttons and plaid trousers rose from the rustic bench.

"Miss Ness? Excuse the informal surroundings. I have an apartment of my own, but I don't invite people to it unless on preliminary acquaintance they prove worthy. Please sit down."

She sat fast. She said she was glad he would see her. She said he'd probably heard it was about Jerry Eldstrom.

"Ah. Poor, foolish Jerry."

"I understand you're his godfather."

"Godfather. Ambiguous category. I could never figure out the exact nature of its privileges or duties. But, yes, if Jerry has a godfather, I'm it."

"Well, I'm his lawyer," she said.

He took a long time straightening a handkerchief in his jacket pocket. "Couldn't they get a man?"

"They wanted me."

"I'd have helped them out with money so they could afford a man."

She laughed. "I'm very good," she said. "That's why they chose me."

"Ah well, different times, different times," he said with an air of not being convinced. Then he looked up. What could he do for her?

"Tell me about Jerry."

"If you're such a good lawyer"—he wasn't going to let up—"you probably know more about him than I do. I've seen him maybe twice a year in the past couple of years. Anyhow, isn't it obvious he's a damn fool to get himself in a mess like this?"

"Oh, I don't know," she said lightly. "It's Jerry's defense he just stood behind the counter of a hardware store and acted with endearing politeness."

"What's he doing behind that counter in the first place?"

Sun filtered through the wisteria to shine on the brown warts on the back of his hands. "Selling nails in a hardware store—what kind of career is that?"

"He seems to like it."

"Sure he likes it. It's easy. It makes no demands. It involves no concentration. I told him—I told his parents, too—if he got a B average in high school I'd pay for his college. Then if he wanted he could come into my business. Accounting. I have my own firm. Had," he said with no regret. "You know what his average was? Straight C."

She leaned back on the rustic bench. C plus, she didn't say.

"College," he said in his heavy voice. "Why should he bother with college? He can fool around without college. He can get the girls. He's soft, Jerry is. No backbone. No drive. No fight." With each vituperative word, his head wobbled on the wrinkled neck.

"He's fighting now." But even that wasn't true, she thought. Jerry was scared, affable, obedient, grateful. She was the one putting up the fight.

"Downwardly mobile—that's my godson. His father had a perfectly nice little business. Drugstore. It's how I met him. I did their accounting. His mother teaches shorthand, or is it typing, at one of those secretarial schools. Such an energetic couple, I thought. Such spunk. So what does their son turn out to be? A hardware store salesman."

A bee buzzed in front of her, and she waved it away.

"You know what my father did?"

Ah. His own life story: what he's been getting around to. The moralistic tale all elderly men eventually get around to. She shook her head.

"He sold newspapers on a corner. Not in his own stand, something dignified, with cigarettes and magazines and a heater for cold weather. Nothing like that. Northwest corner of two Manhattan streets, that was his place of business. He had to be there at five-thirty, when the papers were delivered. If he wasn't there, someone stole them. No chance of a customer at that hour, but that's when they delivered them. Five-thirty

A.M. Five-thirty till the last paper was sold. He sweltered in summer, froze in winter. And rainy days, don't talk to me about rain. If the papers got wet so no one would buy them, that was his tough luck. When he was sick I took over for him. Me, a skinny twelve-year-old kid. That's how I learned about the big-time life that was out there. Standing on some freezing street corner reading a newspaper."

She felt her heels dig into the moist ground. There was no rushing it. She had to hear it all: the night-school classes, the skimping, the setbacks, the textbooks read by inadequate light in the kitchen because he couldn't turn on the light in the bedroom where his two brothers were asleep. Upward mobility: it was what made this country great, and he, Felix Chubb, exemplified it. This was what was real to him: not the wisteria blooming on the trellis around them, not the smell of pine wafting from below, not the parade of wheelchairs dimly viewed on the adjacent lawn, but those strained hours in the kitchen while the rest of the family slept. His set piece, his favorite recital. But he couldn't impose it on the other residents; they would have their sacred pasts, too. Tap them and it would all come out.

When the determined voice finally stopped, she heard the clink of glasses. The afternoon snack. "Drink it all, that's a good girl," she heard someone say. She moved uncomfortably on the bench. She craved food; that was the humiliating fact. No stopping for lunch, she had told Willis before they set out on the two-hour drive from Mr. Ahearn's house—he could eat while she went about her visit. But your

body betrays you. However your mind is absorbed in
its distress, your body signals its gross need for something to fill it.

"Miss Ness, would you like me to show you around
our grounds?" How people misunderstand your
slightest grimace.

"Well, I really—"

"I know. Old people. You don't want to see them.
Think they look bad, sound bad, maybe even smell
bad. You'd be surprised at what some of us bad-
smelling people do. See that small building over there?
No, this way, through the vines. That's our craft center. Pottery, woodworking, weaving, the works. Can't
say I'm interested, but I do hit a wicked Ping-Pong
ball. Miss Ness, you look surprised. Did you think I
came here because I was sick? Disabled? No, indeed.
When my wife, Elsie, died I thought of what she'd
done all those years. The dusting, the sweeping, the
marketing, the cooking—how did the poor woman
stand it? So I looked around, and this was what I hit
on. Rockhaven Retirement Home. I pay a pretty
penny to live here, but it's worth it. Did you think this
was just a nursing home? What a mistake, Miss Ness.
Oh, someday I'll move up, I know. Or is it down? It's
all available. First the halfway house—we old people
do cling to our euphemisms—then at the last, for an
indefinite period, as they say, the nursing home. I've
given orders for what's to happen when I get to that
stage, but I guess you're not interested in that. Meanwhile here I am. Free. Independent. In a position to
say no. Bible studies, lecture on Asian history, exercise class, discussion group...name me a night and I'll

tell you which of these splendid options I can turn down.''

Yes. Just what his acerbic nature would relish: the opportunity to say no.

''And if the local entertainment palls, I can hop on one of the buses that leave here twice a week and make it into New York for a show or a concert or maybe just to check out the stores. See what they're wearing.'' He smoothed down the lapels of his jacket.

''You mean, if I'd asked you, you could have come to the trial?''

''Want me to get up and dance a jig?''

For a second she couldn't speak. She remembered Jerry: the nursing home won't let him out. You hear of lawyers being bamboozled by their clients, but it couldn't happen to her. Not to Lydia Ness, with her experience, her radiant good will.

''Mr. Chubb, tell me about Jerry's brother.''

He put out his mottled hands. ''What's to tell? Poor Elliott. Born without a brain in his head. Didn't Jerry tell you?''

''Not exactly.'' She waited while a man hobbled in on his walker, saw the two of them, turned ceremonially to go the other way. ''Was he always, um, retarded?''

''Retarded. You better not say that to his mother. She dotes on that boy. In her eyes, he's some kind of little saint.''

''Was he born like that?''

''A simpleton from the first crack out of the box,'' he said with his old man's gratified candor. ''First his mother wouldn't believe it—always the way with parents, isn't it? The little darling is just taking his time. He's special. The doctors don't know what they're talking about when they say that blessed child is slow. Then—maybe it takes four, five years—they expect those same ignorant doctors to pull a miracle. Find the magic formula that's going to turn that pretty retard into a normal five-year-old. Then—this is stage three—they accept it. They find within themselves the courage or maybe you might say the foolishness to accommodate to it. Slow is beautiful. Slow is admirable. Slow is the joy of their life." Perhaps attracted by that fierce voice, Stanley poked his head through the opening of the trellis: Did Mr. Chubb need anything? Mr. Chubb waved him away. "Besides, slow always stays around. Normal sons—they grow up and take jobs and get married and find all kinds of reasons for leaving home. Not that slow kid. He's always there. Little Mr. Sunshine, winning your heart. Spoiling your furniture. Stealing the candy from under you nose. Mama's precious, with her night and day."

She looked over at the natty figure. Whatever routine he followed here, it hadn't affected his mind. His shrewd, biting, opinionated mind. "This Elliott. Does he steal?"

"Mama won't admit it, but he'd do a lot worse if they'd let him."

"How can they prevent it?"

"How? By being with him. By arranging their life so one of them is always with him."

"They never leave him alone?"

"Oh, he slips away. A ten-year-old mind in a man's body, you can't prevent him from sometimes slipping away. He has sly tricks. He has big delusions. He knows the territory.''

''What does he delude himself about?''

''Look here. I've been out of touch for two years. I'm not exactly up to date. But before that, it was Jerry. Poor Elliott's favorite game was to play he was big-brother Jerry. Wear Jerry's clothes. Curl up in Jerry's bed. Sneak in on Jerry's life. He even looks like Jerry. Not the face, of course, how could he? The loose mouth. Those vacant eyes. The look—I can't explain it—that's leering and innocent both. But he's built like Jerry, he walks like Jerry, from the back you'd swear it was Jerry— Anything wrong, Miss Ness?''

''No. Go on.''

''I imagine—of course this is speculation, it's difficult to put oneself into the mind of a man who to all intents and purposes doesn't have one—but my guess is Jerry represents to him all that he dimly perceives as fascinating, pleasurable, unattainable. Jerry is at once his frustration and the means of easing it.'' He folded his hands on the plaid trousers. ''I don't mean to play psychologist. I did once and it came to nothing.''

''When was that?''

''One time—it was right after Elsie died—I suggested they put him in some kind of program. I'd help them find it, I said. I knew people who knew people. Plenty of good institutions, I said. Then they wouldn't be so tied down.''

''What happened?''

''I got my head handed to me. Where did I get such ideas! They liked being tied down. It was their pleasure to be on guard. They took satisfaction in knowing that if they took their eyes off him for a second, their simple saint would raise holy hell. No, Miss Ness, they didn't say that. But that's what it amounts to.''

She sat silent. In some distant garden, a firecracker exploded, and then another.

"I don't know. We never had a child, Elsie and I. If we'd had a kid like Elliott, maybe I'd be the same way. Maybe,'' he said with cool disdain. "Do you have a family, Miss Ness?''

"One girl. Three years old.''

"Excuse me for asking—she's not retarded, is she?''

"No. Oh, no. Just the opposite. She's very bright. She's perfect,'' Lydia said.

"Well, a bright three-year-old. Pretty too, doubtless, if she resembles her mother. So you don't know the ache involved in facing a tough dilemma.''

She pulled up a piece of grass and sucked it.

"Miss Ness, I know I'm not supposed to ask this. A defense lawyer—this is the way I understand it— does the best for his, excuse me, her client no matter what. But I'm getting on in age. I don't talk to anyone. I sit like an idiot watching television like everyone else in this place. So tell me this. Do you think Jerry did it? Raped a girl and killed her?''

When she turned, she met his demanding gaze. The first one who had posed the question, she thought. The others by their statements had all implicitly answered it: I know a nice/polite/affable/gentle fellow like Jerry could not have done such a thing. But in fact they didn't know. There was no way they could positively know. No one can be sure about the aberrations into which the nicest, politest, most affable man can be inadvertently led. But only Mr. Chubb had the temerity, the gutsy candor, to formulate the doubt. Only he admitted the question was a viable one.

She rubbed her hand along the rough bark. "No. I really don't think he did it."

For an instant, he closed his eyes. "It wasn't Jerry?"

"I believe it wasn't."

"Well, then, will you be able to get him off?"

"Even though I'm a woman?" She couldn't resist the dig.

The wrinkled face broke into its first smile. "Do your best," he said. "It's true he's disappointed me, but I still wouldn't care to think of my godson in jail for that nasty thing." He stood when she did and asked again if he could show her around. "Some of it is quite admirable, you know. Especially the main house over there. It was once an old hotel—one of the great old hotels. I know what you imagine it must be like inside, but you're wrong, Miss Ness. Quite wrong. You would not see anything to offend you."

How does he know what she imagined? He's right, but how does he know?

"As for my rooms, which are in a wing you can't see from here, I'd like you to see them, too. Comfortable and also stylish. I've stayed in motels across the country, and my little suite at Rockhaven beats any of them."

She had to smile. So she's passed. Having made her acquaintance, he finds her worthy enough to be invited.

Well, she found him worthy, too. He was cantankerous and snobbish and caustic, he probably gave no pleasure to the other residents as they went off to their weaving or pottery or lectures on Asian history, and doubtless he had put the late Elsie through her hoops, but she found him worthy. It was with real regret that she said she had no time for a tour.

No time: that was correct. Back in the car, she told Willis what their next stop would be: a men's clothing store. He should keep his eyes open, and despite its being a holiday, they were sure to find one open in these bustling towns. And after that, she outlined their second stop, which would entail her sitting in the car while Willis conducted the business. She looked at her watch. Traffic was heavy on the hot sunny roads; nine o'clock at the earliest before they could make it home, and her solitary torment would begin again.

FIFTEEN

SHE HAD KNOWN suspense in the past, of course she had. Will the tumor turn out malignant or benign, will the college admissions office say yes, did I pass the bar exam? But these are suspenseful interludes to be got through with anesthetizing therapies. You scrub the floor, you cut your hair, you go running past the point of physical endurance.

Such comfort was out of the question now. At the start of the second night without her child, Lydia sat immobile while her thoughts ran in two opposite directions. One partook of ecstasy. She's safe. Those basically decent people are taking good care of her. They've told her it's all right if she doesn't like the fruit tart for dessert, how about some chocolate—oh, vanilla?—okay, vanilla ice cream. They had found her a pair of blue pajamas that almost fit, and when she's still awake at ten, kindly arms pick her up and rock her. They find themselves unable to resist her imperturbable composure, her particular secretive charm.

The other direction to which she compelled herself was sternly despairing. She's gone. You're not going to see her again. If you face that fact now, steel yourself to its inevitability, it will be easier for you when the time comes. So start rehearsing the necessary ramifications. You're deciding not to go through the saccharine falsity of a funeral. To resist the temptation to cling to relics, you're disposing immediately of her clothing. You're forcing yourself to pen answers to the condolence letters. That's it, right at that desk you sit writing the cheap inanities. And you stiffen yourself with the banal admonitions. Other people get through tragedy. They manage. Look what happens all the time. The truck smashes into the sidewalk where they're playing hopscotch. The lifeguard neglects for an instant to keep watch. The surgeon's hand slips. Why should you consider yourself exempt?

The troubling thing was, she got them mixed up. Though she knew the second course was more salutary, more calculated to effect a cure, her mind kept slipping away from it; she sternly admonished herself, and she also allowed herself the palliative of fantasy. At the same time as she saw herself handing over to Goodwill the plastic bag with the pink sunsuits, she felt her hand stroking Addie's silky hair. Such weakness. Such self-indulgence.

She did move finally. She lay down with her clothes on around midnight. Later she knew she must have slept and woken and slept because when she woke again at four she was in a nightgown. In her dazed state, she had defied the superstition that mandates discomfort to placate fate. Willis was due to call for her at eight, but she was downstairs an hour before that. She stood far back in the lobby so she wouldn't have to engage in the usual cheery talk with the doorman. Then in the car, she explained to Tony that she hoped he'd excuse her, she wasn't up to talking.

He gave his understanding nod. The day she was going to give her summation, such a monumental performance, so dramatic, naturally she'd be wanting to put all her thoughts on that.

She made a great effort. "Tony, listen. It won't be exactly like that. I mean, there won't be the summation right away, the procedure might be changed. Forgive me. I just can't explain right now."

The explanation, in fact, waited till she and Martin Clay were before the judge. She talked earnestly, forcefully, while the expressions on their faces turned from puzzlement to skepticism to amazement to wary approval—Clay, rightfully suspicious, took longer to arrive at this last. "Well, it's in my discretion certainly," the judge said at last. "So go to it, Miss Ness."

She looked around at the courtroom. The usual complement in that adversarial first row: mother, father, three sisters, one brother, the not-unfriendly brother-in-law, all motionless. No patting of shawls or passing of candy today. And on the other side, Jerry's father, his freckled hands on his knees, his face wearing its expression of grave politeness. But scattered empty seats behind them, and no special attentiveness; in the third row, a woman crackled paper as she opened a sandwich, in the fourth row, the two old men sat with eyes half-closed, heads lolling, and in the last row a couple she'd never seen before gave toys to two small children—perhaps they had wandered into the wrong courtroom. "I'd like to recall my own client, Mr. Eldstrom, as a witness," she said.

Jerry had been seated with his chin resting on his palm. Now he raised it. He looked at her and frowned. The diffident frown of one informed by a customer that the polyurethane sealer didn't perform as promised.

"Up here, Mr. Eldstrom," she said as though he needed to be shown where the witness chair was.

He sat gingerly. Then he turned on her his usual half smile with its message of trust and good will: whatever Miss Ness said.

Lydia cleared her throat. She disliked surprises; she especially disliked being the one to administer them. All her life she had campaigned against surprise parties; she considered them an affront to the recipients' sensibilities, an unfair strain on their emotional responses. She wished there were some way to make this more palatable for Jerry, at the same time as she silently affirmed her decision that this was the only way.

Okay, let's get going. "Mr. Eldstrom, I'd like you to think back to the afternoon when you drove Pam home from Neils' Hardware Store. Do you remember it?"

"Well, sure."

"As you reconstructed it for this court, Pam waited outside on the street, and you drove around from the parking lot behind the store to pick her up."

"That's right."

"She had two heavy cans of paint, am I correct?"

"Primer," he gravely corrected her.

"Yes. Primer." She saw the stenographer's hands alert over the keys. "Now, this is my question. When you went back to get your car in the lot, was anyone else in it?"

Jerry gasped. He stiffened. The leg that had been lightly swinging came to a sudden halt. "I...that is..."

"Jerry, you're under oath," she said softly—did the stenographer get it? "Mr. Eldstrom, let me repeat my question," she said in a louder voice. "Was anyone in the car?"

"Yes."

"Who was it?"

"My brother."

Like pulling teeth. "What brother, Mr. Eldstrom?"

"I only have one."

"Ah. And could you tell us about him?"

"His name is Elliott."

"Go on, please. His age, anything you think pertinent."

"He's nineteen. Couple of years younger than me."

"What does he look like?"

"He's built like me. My height and weight. I don't think we really look alike." The pleasant voice quivered a little.

"Anything else, Mr. Eldstrom?"

"He's, that is, Elliott is a little slow."

"What do you mean by slow?"

"He doesn't learn things." Jerry sounded slow himself: a man pained by the probings of inquisition. Lydia took a step backward, as if to give him room. She takes Addie to a doctor who provides lollipops, fits his office as a wonderland of toys, tells jokes as he administers shots: the modern medico. Now she thought of the doctor of her own youth. Gruff, hard-working, stern, competent. "Come on, it's for your own good," he would bluntly say, as he held the needle over the quivering arm. It's for your own good, Jerry, she silently whispered.

"You mean Elliott is retarded?"

"That's what some people call it."

"I see. And what was he doing in your car that day?"

"Hiding."

Without turning, she knew more of the seats were occupied. How does it happen, that silent communication that informs people that now may be the time to leave off gabbing in the lobby and slip into the courtroom? As incomprehensible as the mechanism that sends a message from the head of a column of ants to its rear that an enemy is approaching, it's time to beat a retreat.

"You mean, he didn't come to the store and announce that he was there?"

"No. Oh, no."

"Why not?"

"He knew I'd be angry."

"You don't encourage him to come when you're working?"

Jerry grimly set his lips. "He's not supposed to come at all."

"Well, this day, when he came, how'd he get there?"

"He can make out with buses all right. He knows the way from Pendil Park."

"Does he do that often? Come to visit you at home or your work place?"

"He never does. That is, only when they're not watching."

"Who is they?"

"My parents." Jerry's gaze went to that front-row seat where his father sat and then pulled edgily back.

"You mean, they watch him all the time?"

"One of them."

"Why is that, Mr. Eldstrom?"

Jerry's whole face had undergone an alteration. The salesman smile, the innate diffidence, the eager courtesy—gone. Looking at him—the slack lower lip, the hooded eyes, the head that was not quite upright— Lydia found herself thinking, Now I know what Elliott looks like. "Why is that?" she repeated sharply: Come on, Jerry, pull yourself together.

"They don't want him to do anything bad," Jerry said.

"Bad like what?"

"Whatever you do if you don't have brains."

Hearing that bitter voice, she paused. She had been an only child; she couldn't measure the depth of sibling feelings. If it's your brother, how guilty do you feel? How much, during the years of growing up, is your pleasure in your own virility and competence marred? How often, looking at the shambling figure across the dining table, do you think, There but for the grace of God?

"Can you tell us anything he ever did, Mr. Eldstrom?"

"He stole my car and bumped into someone."

"When was this?"

"High school," Jerry said curtly.

"How'd he get the keys?"

"I don't know. He has tricks."

"What happened after he bumped that car, Mr. Eldstrom?"

"Nothing happened. I mean, I cleaned the biology lab for a month."

"You took the punishment for your brother?"

A nod of the strained head: nothing for the stenographer to write down.

"Can you explain to the court, Mr. Eldstrom, why you assumed the punishment when your brother had done the damage?"

"My mother didn't want them to put him out of the special education class. She thought if he didn't act right they might do that."

When she looked over to the jury for a second, she saw the chef purse his mouth in a noiseless whistle: a man who had not counted on hearing in court about quixotic exploits.

"Anything else bad, as you call it, that Elliott did, Mr. Eldstrom?"

"He killed a dog."

"Had the dog bitten him? Jumped him?" She's in alien territory now. Never ask a question to which you don't know the answer—but she's going on faith, she no more knows the answer to this one than do the spectators behind her, who she feels silently listening, breathing.

"It wasn't like that. It was our neighbors' dog and he untied it and took it for a walk to this field nearby. I don't know why my mother didn't stop him. Maybe she didn't see him. She was watching television. Or cooking. Or ironing. Or she saw him and thought it would be a fun trip for the dog. She didn't know what would happen."

The longest speech he has given so far. "What did happen, Jerry?" Then she heard what she had called him.

"I wasn't there. I only know what he told us later."

"What did he tell you?" Push and pull, push and pull.

Jerry shrugged. "He said he tried to get the dog to fetch for him, like he'd seen it do for Mr. Finley all the time. He threw a stick and said, 'Fetch! Go on, Rusty, fetch!' And the dog wouldn't. It just sat there. It wouldn't obey him. It wouldn't budge. So he got mad. He got frustrated, I guess you'd say. That's when he killed it."

"Killed it how?" she said into the concentrated silence: a whole courtroom out there with the defenselessness of that obdurate dog.

"Do I have to say? Okay. Okay. He tied the dog up and picked up some rocks and bashed the head in."

"What happened to Elliott after that?"

"To Elliott?" His tight face looked up in surprise: why would anything happen to Elliott?

"A dog was killed and no repercussions?"

"Oh, my parents paid the Finleys some money. A lot, I guess—I don't know how much. They asked them not to make a fuss."

"Why was this, Mr. Eldstrom?" A question to which, on reflection, she does know the answer.

"My mother—she's always afraid someone will take Elliott away. Put him in some institution. She likes having him around. He's her boy. She—she loves him."

Lydia thought of Mr. Chubb: Normal kids grow up, take jobs, get married, leave home. "And does she think she's capable of watching over him herself?"

"That's right. That's what she thinks." Until now Jerry had sat motionless, as if the sound of his own voice, droning out one expressionless word after another, exerted some kind of control. But now he began to shake. A trembling that affected his whole body under the light summer suit Miss Ness had suggested that he wear. A court clerk involuntarily moved closer, but the judge leaned forward first: would Mr. Eldstrom like them to call a recess? Jerry gasped and said no. Just if he could have a drink of water. While he was drinking it, she heard—not a commotion, just a rustling from the front row. She kept herself from turning around. When she moved into the apartment house where she now lived and met Pat for the first time, Pat told her about the neighborhood. "Very respectable, but you still have to be careful. You planning to come home alone some nights, honey? Well, let me tell you what you need. No, not a can of Mace, not a gun either, forget that stuff. You just need peripheral vision. So if you're walking straight ahead you can see, without seeming to look, who's behind and what he looks like and what his intentions are." Peripheral vision served her now. It told her that from the front row, the square-jawed husband and one of the sisters had got up; the two of them were edging their way out. For their own reasons, they were leaving the courtroom.

She swallowed the lump in her throat. Anything else Elliott had done, she asked.

"Once he stole my clothes."

"When was this?"

"About a year ago."

"Could you tell the court what happened, Mr. Eldstrom?"

"He got into my apartment at Mrs. Forbes's. Maybe I hadn't locked it, I'm not sure. I was very careful after that."

"What was missing?"

"Two shirts," his sluggish voice said.

"Anything else?" Oh, she's getting to know how she must go after him, probe for the damning detail. "Did Elliott take anything else, Mr. Eldstrom?"

Jerry looked out for a second across the courtroom. "My car keys. My extra set."

"And what'd you do about that?"

"I asked my mother to look through his things. She said she did. She went through his closet and all his drawers. She found the shirts."

"What about the keys?"

"She didn't find them."

"Why do you think that was?"

"He knows how to hide things. Like I said, he has tricks." There was an unaccustomed note in his voice—pain? grudging pride?—and it struck Lydia again what a mix of emotion a man, a boy, would feel about this impaired brother. Anger—of course. Guilt—why not? Resentment at parents who went in for that zealous protection—possibly. All that. But Jerry played the role of protector, too; he must have.

On warm summer nights he said, Come on, kid, let's
go for a ride. In the interval before dinner he took Elliott into the backyard to throw a carefully calibrated
ball. When classmates saw Elliott in the halls and
made the inevitable comments, Jerry masterfully told
them to knock it off. You can't exercise that kind of
protectiveness, that insistent watchfulness, for someone, and not have it translate into a species of caring.
Of love. Elliott was his parents' concern, but in a sense
he was also Jerry's. His life's companion. His unal-
terable burden.

"When you realized that Elliott had your car keys,
Mr. Eldstrom, did you change the locks to your car?"

"I should have. I kept meaning to. But weeks went
by and nothing happened. I just... you know how it
is..."

"Yeah." The sound came from the right, where the
official jury sat. She had forgotten them, so en-
grossed was her mind in that other jury behind her,
from which two members had walked out—was it five
minutes ago? Ten? Dear God, as much as a quarter of
an hour? But now she turned to the twelve men and
women on this court-appointed jury, her eyes as-
sessed them. This was different from the subtle pan-
tomime of satisfaction they had allowed themselves
when Mrs. Lateen showed her colors. Now only the
rug salesman retained his neutral stance; he sat with
hands folded on his knees, eyes straight ahead, as if to
assert his invulnerability to whatever proceedings were
being played out. The others, in varying degrees, had
all overtly succumbed. The accountant blew his nose
in soggy sympathy, the postman—was it he who had

uttered that complicitous "Yeah"?—smacked his knee as if to acknowledge in matters of postponement a similar culpability, the two black women turned on each other a look of unabashed sisterhood. Sitting there, with their concurring murmurs, their participatory gestures, their ratifying nods, they had turned from jury to audience.

"So is it fair to speculate, Mr. Eldstrom"—the show must go on—"that your brother may have had your car keys secreted away for a year?"

Jerry said nothing. He gazed vacantly at the back of the courtroom. "Maybe," he mumbled at last.

At least Lydia thought the word he uttered was—*maybe*. It was hard to hear. More people were coming in, not just crowded into the few remaining spaces at the rear of the courtroom, but up here, where there seemed a steady stream of police officers and court clerks and other messengers between Clay and the judge and the door.

"All right, let's go back to that March afternoon when you drove Pam home. Your brother, as you say, was in the car. Did you introduce them?"

"Well, sure. I mean, I must have. I said, this is my brother Elliott, this is Pam Howells."

"Where were they sitting?"

"Elliott was next to me. She was in back, with those cans."

"Did they talk to each other?"

"No one talked much. She started telling me about stencils she wanted to put on the walls, different designs for stencils, but I told her I wasn't up on that stuff. And Elliott, he doesn't exactly make conversation with girls.''

''What happened when you got to Pam's house?''

''Same as I told you before.'' A touch of testiness in Jerry's voice: a man who on this matter has been right all along. ''I carried in the primer, and she said didn't I want to see what she'd done in her room, and I went up for a minute.''

''Where was Elliott?''

''He waited in the car.''

''Then what?''

''Then I drove him home. I was good and sore; my mother knows he's not supposed to come where I work. She said she just went to a neighbor's for something, and when she came back he was gone. He'd been so quiet lately she had no idea he was going to cut loose. I guess I yelled at her a little and she promised she'd be more careful from then on.''

''Mr. Eldstrom, I have just one more question about that afternoon. You say you told Elliott Pam's last name, and he obviously could have seen her address. From this information, was he capable of ascertaining her phone number?''

Jerry gave a bleak nod. ''Elliott isn't a complete dummy,'' he said. ''He can read a little. Or if he knew the address, he would have the sense to pick up the phone and ask Information.''

When Jerry finished his water, it reminded her how parched her own throat was. Parched and what else? What obstacle was in there, so not a word could emerge? It struck her that it might have been imagination that led her to see two people from that front row walking out. The frenzied imagination attendant on panicked hope. She could turn, of course, and see for herself, but suppose they all were sitting here, a full complement of that inexorable family. Besides, convention mandates that you not turn. When she worked at Legal Aid she had a colleague who used to say that for a woman that was the most onerous part of the job: the prohibition against turning coupled, invariably, with the urge to twitch at a skirt, smooth down a fantasied wrinkle. No actress would put up with it for a second, that aggrieved voice used to say: having to stand so three quarters of the audience sees only that view of your rear.

Lydia turned. Two seats in the front row were empty. "Lydia, you all right?" Tony asked.

She nodded—Yes, fine—and in her dry voice said they had come now to the day of Pam's death. Or, rather, the morning after. As Mr. Eldstrom had testified, he didn't use his car that night, he left it on the street and went to see Fern on foot. Well, when he went to get his car the next morning, was it in the same place as where he'd left it?

"Uh-uh."

"We can't hear you, Mr. Eldstrom." The judge.

"It was halfway down the block," Jerry said. "At least I sort of thought it was down the block. But I wasn't sure. You sometimes forget the exact place where you park."

When Lydia paused for a second, it was Mrs. Lateen she saw. Mrs. Lateen sitting up there on the witness stand, who had been made to look vulgar, mean-spirited, officious, grasping, but who, now that you thought about it, had in effect been right all along. A man walking down the street at eleven-thirty who looked from the rear like Jerry, walked with a little lilt like Jerry, had made it his life's work to resemble Jerry.

Also, she thought, someone who on the phone might have sounded somewhat like Jerry. "Jerry?" That tone of pleased surprise her sisters had reported hearing from Pam had perhaps held more of an element of surprise than they had guessed. "This is Jerry." Is that what Jerry's brother had said on the phone?

And what did he say when she got to the car, this tremulous girl, and Jerry wasn't in it? "Jerry sent me"? "Jerry said he's waiting"? "Hop in and I'll drive you to Jerry"?

Lydia shook her head. With an effort, she brought herself back to the scene on the street: a man finding a car in a slightly different location from the one where he thought he'd left it. "So you did nothing about the car having been moved?"

"Like I said, you can't be sure. Lots of times you don't remember right. Besides, I was in a hurry to get to work. I didn't think about it until later."

"What did happen later, Mr. Eldstrom?" she asked softly.

Jerry looked up, as if to let the whole courtroom see his open face. So open and uncomplicated, it seemed featureless. A face that was just an expression: how did I let myself get into a spot like this? Glum perplexity. "The police came to the store at lunchtime. They said I should come with them."

"Then what?"

"They told me my rights and searched me and told me what happened. They said I could make a call. So I called my parents."

When she followed Jerry's glance, she saw that Mr. Eldstrom was standing, preparing to move out. "Oh, Mr. Eldstrom, I think you should stay and hear this," she said. Irregular, but a certain irregularity had by now infected the whole courtroom. Still more people were standing in back, and more bustling went on to and from the prosecutor's table, and the judge seemed disinclined to limit either of these unaccustomed developments.

"My parents came right away," Jerry said without prodding. "They looked terrible. My father was sort of gray. My mother's eyes were red, but she wasn't crying when she saw me. She said no one could prove anything about me because I didn't do anything. I was innocent. Innocent men can't be found guilty. Besides, I had this alibi. I was at Fern's. Fern would swear it."

When he paused, she thought of that moment in her office when she'd sketched for him the dangers. "You mean that I'll be convicted! Me, Jerry Eldstrom!" Poor, confused man, credulous, ill-advised, unprepared for the actuality.

"My mother said I should just not mention Elliott, not even hint that I had a brother, and it all would work out all right. She swore they would keep him locked up from then on. She said if they took Elliott away, they'd put him in shackles and a straitjacket, that's how he'd be for the rest of his life. She said if that happened she would kill herself. Yes. She would definitely kill herself.''

Above the predictable murmurs, she heard someone sobbing. The accountant? Someone in that front row? No, the black housewife—she sat with eyes streaming. Three daughters, eight grandchildren, the woman had said during the voir dire. Well, suppose one of those grandchildren was, as they say, a little slow. Oh, Mom, how about you keep the little nut for us so we can get out for a change? his mother would say. The woman would hold the little nut in her lap, she would clasp his hand tight as they crossed the street to the playground. When Lydia averted her eyes, it was to see Tony leaving the courtroom.

''It worked out like they said,'' Jerry went on without being asked; he too seemed to have forgotten the regular procedures. ''They indicted me, and then they let me out on bail. The lawyer arranged that. Some lawyer my parents knew about. Then my father heard about the Lyttle office and he said we should change— Well, you know about that.''

''You''—he was speaking to her now. His apologia to Miss Ness, who had put up a fight for him. ''I never lied,'' he said. ''I never actually said anything that wasn't true. If anyone had asked me about Elliott— well, today you did ask me.''

Would he wonder how she had found out about Elliott? No. He would take for granted that others had skills, resources, tactics, feats of perception not available to him. He would simply go about his business of aiming to please everyone, and when that proved impossible, he would offer his sincere and diffident apologies. There would always be customers who singled him out from all the others behind the counter, girls who were ready to jump into bed with him, people prone to forgive his ineptitude because of his pleasant manners and easy smile.

The murmurs of the crowd got louder—a roar from the back rows, where people were standing. "Out of my way," someone shouted. "Not in this row," another called out. She saw the judge beckoning to her, but Tony got to her first. "Here, Lydia. This just came. Your secretary called in to say I should give you this."

"This" consisted of a short note: "Someone named Diane called and said you should get this message right away. She wants you to know that Addie just appeared and is fine, but she says where's she been and what the hell is going on?"

A small sheet of paper, a scrap, really, which is what Tony must have found in his pocket when he was called as Miss Ness's assistant to the phone and on which he had dutifully written while leaning over some stranger's desk, but her hand stroked it and stroked it, smoothing out the creases, caressing the coarse sheet with the tender touch she might have used for a child's delicate skin. Then she realized the judge was talking.

"I want to announce to this courtroom that Mr. Clay has just informed me he has moved to dismiss the charges. It is a move in which I heartily support him." He cleared his throat. "May I add, for the benefit of those who are personally involved in this case"—his gaze, which had been impartially turned on the courtroom, rested with unmistakably meaningful intent on

the occupants of the front row—"you people should
know that according to word I've just received, Elliott
Eldstrom is now or shortly will be in police custody,
charged with the murder of Pamela Howells. It re-
mains for me only to thank the jury and congratulate
Miss Ness."

"Actually, Your Honor, if I might say a word to the
jury myself." She had put the papers into her skirt
pocket, but her fingers had no intention of letting
them go. "I want to thank the jury, too. You've all
been wonderful—attentive and patient and understanding. And because the developments this morning have been so surprising—surprising to me as well
as you—I just want to talk a second about this trial.
It's been about the loss of a young life. A life that gave
pleasure to lots of people and can never be replaced.
A life that will be mourned for a long time. But in a
way the trial has also been about mothers. What
mothers will do for the sake of their children. The
lengths they'll go to. The risks they'll take. Not just
mothers. Families. Damn. I thought I could get
through it."

"Here's a handkerchief, Lydia," Tony said.

"I think we could all use a drink," the judge said.

"LYDIA, you pulled it off. What a coup." It was Ben
Lyttle; from his explanation, it appeared that he too
had been tuned in to that busy grapevine, and when he
heard what was going on, he wanted, he said, to be in
on the kill.

"I'm not so sure your clients will be overjoyed," she
murmured.

"They will be when they think it over. That hare-brained scheme of theirs—they'll realize they might have got their elder son put away for life. Anyhow, I was looking at the father when you let loose with the facts. He's no dope. Surprise crossed his face, but also, I could swear, relief. Sheer relief that the idiocy at last was over." He took her arm and pressed it.

"But how did you know?" he went on. "What made you act? When you left here Tuesday night, you were plainly headed for an acquittal. Why didn't you leave it at that?"

When Ben's exuberant voice boomed this out, they were standing at the low partition that separates spectators from participants. Immediately behind them, rigid, unmoving, were the Howells family. The mother still wrapped in her black lace badge of misery, the father with his gaunt cheeks and sunken eyes, three sisters, a brother. Also, at the very end, the square-faced brother-in-law who had walked out and attended to his mission and now was back. In their battle for vengeance, these people had performed an appalling act. Theirs was the kind of battle in which victory brings no exhilaration and a finale provides no peace. Sitting in the seats they had made their own, they looked drained, dazed, empty.

Except now something was to break through the daze. What made Miss Ness act? As Lyttle said this, the figures behind her stiffened. What would Miss Ness now divulge? What accusations would she make? What further trouble did she have it in her power to inflict?

She didn't answer for a second. A couple of jury members—the postman, the accountant—stood patiently in a pose that said it would appease their curiosity to talk to her, and she gave the signal that said, Just a minute. Then she waved at Tony, whose beaming face and incomprehensible words issued from across the table. Then she looked at Ben. "Why did I act? I don't know. I just had an idea something was wrong. Some anomaly. So before Clay got at it, I decided to check it out."

A collective sigh went through the row. Safe. Whatever they had done, and then in response to a phone call precipitously undone, there would be no investigation. Miss Ness was going to drop it. No one would badger them with questions.

She and Ben waited while they now walked out. As you wait at a funeral: let the chief mourners go first. Papa holding on to Mama, who was supported by Maureen, whose elbow was steered by the brother, who made a gesture of weary impatience as the red-haired sister dropped her bag and fumbled for it beneath the chairs. She never wants to talk to them, never wants to see them again. She has no wish to receive their thanks or their apologies or their justifications, or whatever defense their distorted and tormented minds see fit to deliver. And she surely doesn't want to expose to them her suffering, let them even vicariously participate in it. She wants to erase them. Their rolls of candy, their gratuitous bustling, their stricken eyes, their small, pouting mouths.

At the same time, she knows they are united. Bound by terrible, close ties. Part of each other's lives forever.

Ben was waiting. Try again: What made her act? "I looked over my notes and it struck me. He never let me talk to anyone from his youth. Not the high school principal, not some old family friend. He'd mention them and then pull back. 'Don't bother,' he said. Or, 'They won't want to talk.' Or, 'They won't know anything.' And sure enough, two people both mentioned that unfortunate Elliott."

"Did you go to see Elliott yourself?"

"No. I bought a present, a man's sweater, and had Willis bring it in. Just to make sure he was really there."

"Why the restraint?"

"I didn't want to alert them. Jerry especially. I didn't know what wild invention he and his parents might cook up if they had time to think it over. This way I'd be getting the story before those poor demented people made a stab at altering it."

"You took a big risk not getting Elliott in custody first."

Her hand went once more to the paper in her pocket. "I took a lot of risks," she said, and for a second she thought of those involved, without consent, in that risk taking. Doug. Pat. Even Owen. What a lot of explaining she was going to have to do. To her dependable friend Pat. To that stalwart Doug. Even to Owen with his muddled plans and doomed hopes.

"One more question. How did you know Elliott had been in the car that time Jerry drove the girl home from the store?"

"He made a slip. His only slip. He said, 'I wanted to get him home fast.' Then he explained that the 'him' referred to a frozen turkey. It was also his only lie, now that I think about it. But there was something off-key—I should have picked up on it then. I'd have saved a lot of suffering," she added slowly.

"Hey, Lydia, no talk like that. You were brilliant. Sensational." Ben stood alert, conscious of the reporters who had recognized his bushy hair and resonant voice, and were beginning to crowd around. "I understand there's champagne back at the office. They're arranging a party."

"Thanks, Ben, but save it. Right now there's a private party I have to get to."

A J.K.G. Jantarro Mystery

WORK FOR A DEAD MAN

First Time in Paperback

SIMON RITCHIE

JANTARRO DIDN'T LIKE TO LOSE A CLIENT...
ESPECIALLY NOT TO A MURDERER.

When megabuck film producer/director Alan Laki is poisoned, private investigator J.K.B. Jantarro takes special interest. He'd been hired by Laki to investigate the bizarre spending behavior of the man's gorgeous wife, Camelia. But now Laki's been murdered, his empire is in chaos and Jantarro is working for a dead man.

As for motives, Camelia Laki had millions of them... all dollar bills. Toss in a greedy business partner, a gossip columnist and her guilty secret, a hothead and a resentful brother-in-law, add three goons with homemade baseball bats, and it's lights...camera...action, as Jantarro plays the lead in a script full of scheming passion, dirty deals and death.

"**Ritchie deftly blends literate writing, a light touch of humor, a likeable hero and memorable characters for a terrifically suspenseful tale.**"

—Publishers Weekly

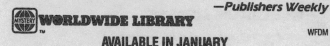

WORLDWIDE LIBRARY

WFDM

AVAILABLE IN JANUARY

From the author of the highly acclaimed
Father Dowling novels now seen on ABC-TV

RALPH McINERNY

AN ANDREW BROOM MYSTERY

BODY AND SOIL

First Time In Paperback

TILL DEATH DO US PART...

After nearly thirty years of unhappily ever after, Wyler, Indiana's most affluent and argumentative couple decided to call it quits. At least Pauline Stanfield did. Hal Stanfield knew a divorce would unearth secrets—both the financial and extramarital kind—he preferred to keep buried.

But when Hal is found bludgeoned to death in his kitchen, attorney Andrew Broom finds himself defending a wife suspected of choosing murder over divorce. Soon he discovers that even the best-laid plans of marriage—or murder—can go dangerously awry when a twisted killer decides to play judge, jury... and executioner.

"*Body and Soil* confirms McInerny's mastery
of the light mystery." —*Publishers Weekly*

WORLDWIDE LIBRARY

BAS

AVAILABLE IN JANUARY

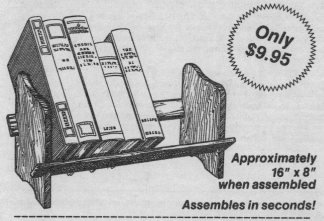